Demon Princess

REIGN OR SHINE

MICHELLE ROWEN

Walker & Company
New York

ACKNOWLEDGMENTS

Thank you to Stacy Cantor, editorial princess, whose magic red pen royally helped this book.

Thanks to all of my friends, online and off, for your support and continued encouragement of my writing. You all rock!

First published in the United States of America in 2009 by
Walker Publishing Company, Inc.
Visit Walker & Company's Web site at www.bloomsburyteens.com

For information about permission to reproduce selections from this book, write to Permissions, Walker & Company, 175 Fifth Avenue, New York, New York 10010

Library of Congress Cataloging-in-Publication Data
Rowen, Michelle.
Demon princess : reign or shine / Michelle Rowen.
  p.   cm.   — (Demon princess ; 1)
Summary: In small-town Canada after her mother's fourth marriage, sixteen-year-old Nikki learns that her long-lost father is king of the demons, a fact that threatens to destroy her newfound popularity and sense of belonging.
ISBN-13: 978-0-8027-9534-2 • ISBN-10: 0-8027-9534-X (paperback)
ISBN-13: 978-0-8027-8492-6 • ISBN-10: 0-8027-8492-5 (hardcover)
[1. Demonology—Fiction. 2. Popularity—Fiction. 3. High schools—Fiction.
4. Schools—Fiction. 5. Remarriage—Fiction. 6. Moving, Household—Fiction.
7. Canada—Fiction.] I. Title.
PZ7.R7963Dem 2009   [Fic]—dc22   2009000205

Book design by Nicole Gastonguay
Typeset by Westchester Book Composition
Printed in the U.S.A. by Quebecor World Fairfield
2 4 6 8 10 9 7 5 3 1 (paperback)
2 4 6 8 10 9 7 5 3 1 (hardcover)

All papers used by Walker & Company are natural, recyclable products made from wood grown in well-managed forests. The manufacturing processes conform to the environmental regulations of the country of origin.

To Jim McCarthy,
my prince of an agent

1

"That guy is staring at you."

I glanced over at the far right corner of the cafeteria and groaned. Melinda was right. In fact, I knew the tall, dark-haired guy in the faded Van Halen T-shirt and navy blue hooded sweatshirt had been staring at me for about ten minutes and I was relieved someone else had noticed.

"Who is he?" I asked. "I don't recognize him from around here."

"No idea. Some loser."

"Just ignore him," I suggested.

She grinned at me before taking a sip from her bottle of Evian, the sum total of her Wednesday lunch. "Maybe he wants to ask you to Winter Formal."

I made a face. "No, thank you."

"Well, he's going to be too late." Her grin widened. "Because I know who *is* going to ask you."

I blinked. "Who?"

She shrugged. "Can't tell. It's a secret. But not for long."

Great. A secret. I felt my blood pressure shoot up about fifty points right then, wondering who she was talking about.

Melinda looked way too proud of herself. She couldn't possibly know how much stress she was causing me with her cryptic statements. She didn't have any comprehension of what a loser I'd been before transferring to Erin Heights High School two months ago—not that I felt all that much different now. Though I'd seriously lucked out when I'd become friends with her.

Not only did my mom move us three thousand miles away from our old home in San Diego, but she'd moved us right out of the *country*. We were now settled in the small town of Erin Heights, which was about thirty minutes west of Toronto, in Canada, nestled right next to Lake Ontario. Mom had been born in the area so she was excited to be back. Me? Not so much.

And it was cold here. Like, *cold*. I knew it was only like this during the winter months, but unfortunately, being that it was the seventh of December, one day after my not-so-sweet sixteenth birthday, we still had a whole lot of winter left to shovel our way through. Snow should be for skiing over on vacation, not for trudging through in less-than-adequate shoes on your way to school. That was my opinion, anyway.

I hadn't been in a very good mood when we arrived in October. In fact, "miserable" probably would have best described me. I had to start school while the semester was already in progress—the absolute kiss of death for someone trying to fit in.

Mom got married to Robert, a Canadian accountant she met on a singles cruise, and we moved up here right after the honeymoon. I probably should be used to this kind of thing by now, though. My mother's been married *four* times, and I've had to start at a different school each and every time. Since I'd never had much of a chance to settle in and get to know people who already had established cliques and friendships, I was usually out of luck.

Nikki Donovan: *outcast*. Welcome to my life.

The first day I moseyed into Erin Heights High I was expecting exile. Up until lunchtime my first day, it was exactly that. I was ignored. I got some curious stares, a few unfriendly glares, but nothing too major.

I ate my oh-so-gourmet peanut-butter sandwich alone and seriously considered dwelling eternally in my morbid unhappiness for lack of anything better to do.

But then Melinda James and her entourage entered the room and sat down in the very center of the cavernous cafeteria. I had overheard a couple of classmates referring to them as the "Royal Party," and at first glance I could tell that Melinda was the queen. Pretty, blonde, stuck-up, and wealthy—a total high school cliché. Or at least that was my first impression of her.

The reason that we were best friends two months later was quite simple.

Five minutes after she walked into the cafeteria that day she nearly choked to death on a honey-mustard pretzel.

I was clued in that something was wrong when everyone around her started to freak out and I turned, curious to see what was happening.

Melinda had her hands around her throat and she was

making odd little noises. Everyone thinks that when you choke on something you cough, but when you're choking, no air is getting down your throat so, actually, no coughing. Her face was quickly turning blue. Her perfectly smooth long hair was messy from tossing her head back and forth. Her model-pretty face wore an expression of terror. And everyone in her general vicinity had taken one rather large step away from her.

No one knew how to save her. No one was even willing to try.

Well, except for me. Thanks to being forced by my mother to take a CPR class the previous summer, I knew the Heimlich maneuver. When I approached, Melinda stared up at me with wide, watery eyes. Her lips had quickly developed a distinctive purple tinge.

Without saying anything first—it wasn't exactly the time for friendly introductions—I grabbed her designer shirt, spun her around, and tried my best not to break any of her ribs. The offending piece of honey-mustard pretzel flew out of her mouth and hit a guy named George Rodriguez, who I'd later learn was the president of the chess team, squarely in the forehead.

George wasn't too thrilled about the situation. But Melinda was grateful. *Very* grateful.

"You are my guardian angel," she said very seriously, with her hand against her throat. "Uh . . . who are you?"

"I'm Nikki," I said nervously. "Nikki Donovan."

"You saved my life."

"It's no big deal."

"It *is* a big deal. Huge." She took a drink of water with shaking hands. "You're new here?"

"Brand new. This is my first day."

"So you don't know anybody yet. You were over there eating alone, right?"

I looked down the table of Royal Party members—the most popular kids at school—all staring at me as though I'd done something miraculous. I really hated being the center of attention. "I haven't met too many people yet. No."

"Then consider yourself my new best friend," she said. "For a week. I can introduce you to everybody and help you fit in here. And you can sit at this table at lunch. Does that sound okay?"

I shook my head. My mouth felt dry. "Forget it. It's really not necessary."

Her eyes widened a little, possibly with surprise that I hadn't jumped on her offer right away. "Come on. One week. You *have* to say yes."

I *had* to?

I chewed my bottom lip as I considered my options. Basically, be alone and try valiantly to make friends with people who already had established cliques that year, or take Melinda up on her one-week offer of friendship and try to make the best of it.

"Okay," I finally agreed, careful not to get my hopes up too much that it would lead to a real friendship.

The other members of the Royal Party mostly ignored me or kept their distance, which was fine by me because they were kind of intimidating. But the more I hung out with Melinda as the days went by, the more I realized that she wasn't all that scary. Since I had a really hard time faking being nice—I wasn't much of an actress, I guess—I just behaved like myself. Warts and all.

I don't *actually* have any warts. It's just a saying.

After the week was over, I assumed that was it—I'd be on my own again. But Melinda kept chatting with me by the lockers after school like nothing had changed.

"Isn't my week up?" I asked her plainly.

She looked at me with confusion for a moment. "Your week?"

"My allotted week to hang out with you."

Slow realization came over her face. "Oh. You mean you don't want to be my friend anymore?"

Now I was the confused one. "You said I could spend time with you for a week. The week's over."

She waved a hand. "That was just the screening process. I wasn't sure if you would try to use me or not."

I blinked. "Do a lot of people use you?"

"You'd be surprised." She shrugged. "I only realized it recently—it became, like, crystal clear to me—that at least half my so-called friends aren't really my friends. They usually try to use me for what they think I can get them—popularity, hot guys, you name it. So they flock. Therefore, my friendship screening process recently came into effect."

"And I passed?"

"With flying colors." She grinned. "So, can we be friends? For real?"

I could have been wrong, but I swear I saw a glimmer of doubt in her eyes, as if she half-expected me to say no. Melinda James—the queen of the Royal Party—scared I wouldn't want to be her friend?

I hadn't even thought it was possible, but at that moment I could admit to myself that, yeah, I did want to be Melinda's friend. I'd realized over the week that we had a lot in common. I mean, she was perfect and I was far from it. But we liked the same movies, television shows, books. We'd talked for hours one night about absolutely nothing. I felt comfortable with her.

"Friends," I agreed with a smile. "For real."

And that was that.

Suddenly I had a chance to fit in somewhere and be accepted after sixteen years of being a big nobody. I hadn't asked for it, but being friends with Melinda was like winning the social-life lottery.

Which apparently included being stared at by a really strange guy with shoulder-length dark hair that hid his face so I couldn't even see what he looked like.

He was starting to seriously creep me out.

Melinda eyed me. "He's bothering you, isn't he?"

"Forget it."

But she didn't forget it. She stood up instead, and everyone along the cafeteria table stopped eating and talking long enough to turn and look at her.

"Hey, loser!" she shouted in the guy's general direction. "Why don't you take a picture of her? It'll last longer."

I felt my cheeks heat up. "Melinda—" I pulled at her arm, then glanced over to see the guy shove his hands in the pockets of his jeans and walk out of the cafeteria.

She smiled. "See? You just have to be more confrontational."

"If you say so." I glanced back at the entrance and this time my breath caught in my chest because at that very moment, Chris Sanders walked in.

Picture: hot, gorgeous, fabulous, wonderful, and popular. Dark blond hair, blue gray eyes like the ocean on a stormy day, broad shoulders, and a killer smile. A whole year older than me. Total perfection.

That was Chris.

He was my major crush since I'd started at Erin Heights, and since he was also a member of the Royal Party, I'd had the chance to talk to him a few times. Every time I'd tried very hard to hold back the drool.

"Here he comes." Melinda grabbed my hand. "Just try to stay calm."

My eyes widened and I turned to look at her. "He's not the one you were talking about, is he?"

She gave that noncommittal shrug. "Maybe."

"And did you have anything to do with this?"

"I might have helped a little bit." She grinned. "I figure you've been here two months. It's about time for you to start dating somebody worthy of your new social status. Besides, it's only two days till the dance and you still haven't accepted anyone else's invitation."

No, I hadn't. A couple of guys had asked me, but I

wasn't interested in any of them. I'd planned on skipping the dance altogether.

Chris Sanders was going to ask me to Winter Formal? *Me?*

If that was the case then I'd seriously have to reconsider my decision.

I inhaled so sharply that I almost had a coughing fit. Luckily, I didn't. That wouldn't have made a very good impression on the hottest guy in school, who was getting closer to me with every step he took.

I forced myself to be cool. It was a struggle.

"Hey, Nikki," he said as he approached the table.

"Hey," I squeaked as if I'd been chewing on a helium sandwich.

His gaze flicked to the very amused Melinda and then back to me. "Can I talk to you?"

"Uh-huh." Another squeak.

His dazzling smile widened. "Let's go out in the hall. If that's okay."

"Sure." I slid out from behind the table and followed him to the hallway, right next to a long bank of lockers that I leaned against to give the illusion of casual confidence. I wished Melinda had given me some kind of warning so I could have worn something nicer than black jeans and my old blue cable-knit sweater. At least my ankle boots had heels. Since Chris was tall—and I wasn't—it helped a bit.

"I want to ask you something," he began. "I know this is last minute, but I'd really like you to go to Winter Formal with me. If you want to."

And there it was.

Since I was completely stunned, I didn't say anything for a moment. I think he took that to mean I wasn't sure how to answer.

His smile faded a bit around the edges. "I mean, I know we don't know each other very well, but I think you're really cool. And pretty. And you'd be great to hang out with. But if you're not interested, I totally understand—"

"No." I cut him off. "I'm interested. I'm definitely interested. I'd love to go to the dance with you."

The smile returned. "Well, good. I've got a limo and everything lined up."

"That'll do nicely." I grinned at him.

A limo. Wow. I knew that Chris's father was a big-time lawyer in Toronto and his mother was a doctor. They definitely didn't have to worry about money.

My mom, on the other hand, wrote romance novels. The non-office freedom of her job helped when she had to make her sudden marriage moves around North America. As long as she had her laptop she could write from anywhere. But my father? I had no idea what he did for a living. I'd never known him. He'd left my mom when she was still pregnant with me.

"This is good," Chris said. "I've wanted to ask you out since you moved here. I guess I was worried you'd say no."

I almost laughed out loud at that. Who in their right mind would say no to Chris Sanders?

"Well, then I guess it's good that I said yes."

"It is." He put his hand against the locker next to my head and leaned in toward me. He was so close now that I could feel the warmth from his body. "And I wanted to tell you something else, but I'm a day late."

"What's that?" I breathed. His mouth was only inches away from mine.

"Happy birthday."

"You know it was my birthday yesterday?"

He nodded. "Did you have a good one?"

"There was cake. Chocolate."

"That sounds exciting."

"It was," I said with mock seriousness. "It really was."

"Well, happy birthday, Nikki." He leaned closer and kissed me.

I was *kissing Chris Sanders*. I'd dreamed about this so many times since I'd moved here, but never thought I'd actually get the chance.

Kissing him. In the public hallway at school.

I could die happily now.

When he leaned back from me, I was about to say something—I wasn't even sure what—when Chris glanced to his left.

"Can I help you with something?" he asked with a frown.

I swiveled around to see that the same guy who'd been staring at me earlier in the cafeteria was down the hall from us.

Staring at me.

Creepy.

He didn't reply to Chris's question. Instead, after a short hesitation, he turned and walked away, exiting the school completely through the doors at the end of the hall.

"He totally interrupted us." Chris looked down at me with a grin. "That's just rude, don't you think?"

"*Very* rude," I agreed, deciding to put whoever he was out of my mind immediately.

"Now, where were we?" he asked.

"Before or after you kissed me?"

"I'm thinking . . . *during*." He bent his head to mine again for another quick kiss before the bell rang, signaling that lunch was over and I had to head to my next class.

By then I had a permanent smile on my face.

I was finally sixteen years old. I had the coolest best friend. A gorgeous, popular guy had just asked me to go to the school dance. *And* he'd kissed me! Everything I'd ever wanted in life was coming to me. I seriously couldn't have asked for anything more.

Now I just had to make sure that nothing spoiled it.

2

I stayed after school to study for an English test I had the next day on *Romeo and Juliet*. When I left at five o'clock it was already dark outside, but I didn't hurry home since I knew nobody was there. Mom and Robert were at his company's Christmas party and wouldn't be back before midnight.

I'd forgotten to wear the hat, gloves, and scarf Mom had given me yesterday as part of my birthday present. The winter chill bit deeply into me as I left school property, but I was in too good a mood to let the subzero temperature bother me.

Well, not much, anyway.

It was a fairly short walk home. Twenty minutes if I went the regular way—up a hill and through a maze of well-populated streets. If I wanted to, I could even hop on the bus that went right past the mall on the way to my new neighborhood. But I'd found a shortcut by walking through a park nicknamed Hungry Hollow, which was at the bottom of a deep ravine and shrouded by thick trees. If I crossed a bridge over a narrow, meandering river, went past a parking

lot—empty at this time of year since it was meant for people using the soccer field during the warmer months—and
past a small kiddies' area with swings and a seesaw, then
up the equivalent of three flights of wooden stairs to get
to ravine-set houses, it was only ten minutes from school
to home. Twelve if I took my time.

I'd walked the same route for two months and hadn't
run into a single problem, except for the odd monster
snowdrift. I always made sure I was fully aware of my surroundings. You never could be too careful.

Unfortunately, today was going to be the exception. I
was in such a good mood after what had happened with
Chris, and I was so caught up in wondering what I was
going to wear to the dance, that I didn't notice somebody
was following me until after I'd fully entered the poorly lit
park. And by then it was too late to change my mind about
the direction I was going in.

With a sick, sinking feeling I realized it was the weird
guy who'd been staring at me in school that day. I recog-
nized the sweatshirt after a quick glance behind me.

Who was he? What did he want?

Maybe nothing, I thought. *Maybe he's just taking the same
route as me. Coincidence only.*

If that was the case, then fine. But if it wasn't . . .

I swallowed hard and picked up my pace. I had a ways to
go before I got to the wooden stairs, but first I reached a big
oak tree and a patch of thick foliage that stood in the center
of the park. As soon as I knew I was out of sight from the
main path, I ducked behind some snow-covered bushes.

The guy stopped in front of the huge tree and turned around with an expression of confusion showing under the dark hood of his sweatshirt. He craned his neck to see where I'd disappeared to. When his gaze reached the bushes, he paused.

He could clearly see my hiding spot. A sharp stab of panic went through me.

He squinted at me. "Nikki Donovan?"

I felt a flare of anger push past my fear. "What do you want?"

"Why are you down there?"

I hissed out a breath and watched the air freeze in front of me. My heart was thudding wildly against my ribs. I didn't want to be the kind of girl who hid from danger or got pushed around. I'd much rather be like Melinda in the cafeteria today—the sort of girl who confronted things head-on without fear. But yelling across a crowded room was one thing. Being followed into a deserted park was another one altogether.

A quick head-to-toe scan of the guy confirmed that he wasn't carrying a knife. Or a gun. In fact, he didn't have anything, not even a winter coat or scarf to keep him warm. I forced myself to stand up and shuffle away from my protective area—which I now realized wasn't very protective at all.

I crossed my arms tightly in front of me. "You shouldn't follow people into dark areas."

"Sorry. I . . . I didn't mean to scare you."

Naturally, I wasn't convinced.

"What do you want?" I asked again, glancing over at the

wooden staircase. I could get to it in less than thirty seconds if I ran fast. I wished my backpack wasn't so heavy, but it was filled with books I needed to finish cramming for my Shakespeare test tomorrow.

"I need to talk to you," he said. "It's urgent."

I swallowed hard. My guard was still up. *Way* up. "Who are you?"

He looked confused. "Who am I?"

"It's not a trick question. What's your name?"

For a second I didn't think he was going to tell me, but then, "Michael. My name's Michael."

I'd been nursing a headache since having the chocolate cake last night and I'd gone all day without any Tylenol. My head was pounding now and getting worse by the minute. "Why are you following me, Michael?"

"I have to talk to you. I tried to earlier, but there were too many people around."

My hands felt like they were freezing into two solid blocks of ice. Maybe it was the cold that was helping to numb my fright a bit. Not a lot, but a bit.

"You should have talked to me at school, anyway. I have to get home now." When I turned to leave, I felt him grab my arm. I froze, and not just with the temperature. I turned to face him, my eyes wide with fear. "Let go of me."

He let go of me immediately and took a step back. "Sorry. It's just that I have to talk to you. There's no time."

"You need to leave me alone."

His jaw tensed. "I can't do that." He stared at the ground and then pushed the dark hair off his face. I finally got a glimpse of what he looked like underneath. I don't know why I'd expected him to be ugly. The fact that he was attractive surprised me, but didn't ease my mind at all.

He wasn't as thin as I'd thought at first glance, more lean and athletic under the ill-fitting clothes. Which would explain the killer grip he had. He had high cheekbones and stern eyebrows like black slashes above his emerald green eyes.

"The cops patrol this park all the time," I told him. "So I think you should leave or there's going to be trouble. I'm going home and I strongly suggest you do the same."

He raised his gaze to look directly at me. "Not yet, Princess."

I blinked at that. "Who are you calling Princess?"

"You." He took a step toward me.

I took a big step back. "You need to stay away from me or we're going to have a serious problem here."

He frowned deeply, then reached into the pocket of the navy blue hoodie he wore. I clenched my fists, trying to ready myself for anything. My throat felt too tight to scream, but I'd give it my best shot.

He pulled out an envelope and offered it to me. I stared at it without moving.

"What's that?" I managed.

"It will explain a little. But you need to come with me right now. He's waiting for us."

"Who's waiting?"

"Your father."

My mouth dropped open. Out of everything he could have said to me, I couldn't have expected that. At all.

"You're obviously mistaken," I said. "I don't have a father."

"You do. Please, take the envelope."

My fear and anger were quickly losing ground to a deep annoyance. "Look, I don't know who put you up to this, but it's not funny."

The hand that held the envelope dropped a little. Michael seemed uncertain of what to do now, since I wasn't being at all agreeable. "He . . . he said you'd be surprised to hear from him after all this time, but there's no other way."

"My *father* sent you to give me a message," I said with major disbelief.

"And to bring you to his side."

I still couldn't believe I was hearing him correctly. "Well . . . why you?"

He frowned. "Because he asked me to."

This was so unreal. I'd barely thought about my father for years. It helped that my mother refused to talk about him even on the rare occasion that I was curious to learn more about where I came from. I guess being left alone and pregnant at eighteen might make you have a tendency to want to forget the somebody who's treated you so badly. Made sense to me.

Michael waited patiently with his arms crossed, the envelope held loosely in his right hand.

"Let me tell you a little something about my father," I said. My headache was getting worse the longer I talked to this weirdo. "He got my mother pregnant and then he disappeared without a trace and left her all on her own. Sixteen years and he hasn't tried to see me. Not once. Not a letter, a phone call, or an e-mail. So even if I did believe you, why would I want to see him at all?"

His face looked strained. "Because there are things you need to know. About him. About you."

My eyes narrowed. "I have an idea. Why don't you take that envelope you have there back to whoever gave it to you and tell them to shove it?"

He raised his eyebrows. "I don't think that message would go over too well."

I had to admit, I'd always imagined what it might be like to have a real father. The four guys my mother had married over the last twelve years hadn't exactly fit the bill for me—and in the end, obviously not for her either. Somebody doesn't get married that many times if they've found Mr. Right.

Robert the accountant was the latest. I didn't like him much. That was an understatement, actually. His hobbies seemed to include yelling a lot and getting mad about stupid things—like when I left my homework on the sofa in front of the television one night. Not exactly anything to freak out over, in my opinion. I really didn't like how he treated me—or my mom, for that matter. Mom said it had only been two months and it might take a bit of adjusting to our new living arrangements. I wasn't so convinced, but I figured I'd try to wait it out.

Still, I'd seen too many of her relationships start out strong, only to fizzle after a couple of years. Sometimes it didn't even take that long for her to realize she'd made a mistake. This was always after we'd already moved across the country, though. Atlanta, Phoenix, San Diego, and now Erin Heights. I was kind of sick of being told what to do and forced to move all over the place. But I didn't really have much of a choice in the matter. I went where I was told to go. I did what I was told to do. I tried not to make too much of a fuss about it. End of story.

But any of the jerks she'd married were better than my biological father. At least I'd seen them with my own eyes. As far as I was concerned, my father didn't even exist.

I was pacing a small section of the park, and when I glared at Michael, it was with anger now, not fear. Why did he have to stir up old issues for me? And after I was having such a great day, too.

He was ruining my good post-birthday mood.

"If you're the delivery boy for my long-lost father," I said, "then tell me. Where is he? Why couldn't he come and see me himself if he's so interested all of a sudden? And why now, after all these years?"

Michael raised his eyes to mine and his expression looked uncertain. Maybe he didn't know. Maybe somebody had given him money to contact me. Strange, but possible.

"You probably won't believe me right away," he said. "But you have to. It's all true."

"Tell me."

"Take the envelope and I'll tell you." He held it out to me again.

I had to take a step closer to him as I snatched it out of his grip. "Fine. Envelope delivered. Now tell me. *Please*."

He took a deep breath in and let it out slowly. "Your father is the king of the Shadowlands."

I blinked slowly. "What is that supposed to mean?"

"The Shadowlands is the dimension that separates this human realm from the Underworld and Hell."

I didn't say anything for a moment. Again, this guy had managed to render me speechless. He certainly wasn't predictable.

"Another *dimension*," I repeated.

"Yes."

"And my father is the king there. In this other dimension."

"That's right."

"And that's the reason why you called me Princess before. Because my father is a king."

He nodded. "You're the current heir to the throne."

My mouth felt very dry and my head throbbed. I rubbed my temples. "You're kidding, right?"

"No, I'm not kidding. I knew you'd have a difficult time believing me; you've lived the life of a human for sixteen years. That's why you have to see your father personally. He'll explain things much better than I will—even though I'm supposed to answer any questions you have to the best of my ability. He wants you to read his letter and then come with me—"

"Let me guess. To the Shadowlands?"

"That's right."

I frowned. "Hold on. Did you say that I've lived a human life for sixteen years? What other kind of life could I have lived?"

He jammed his hands into the pockets of his jeans. "Your father is a demon."

"You're crazy. I'm not listening to this." I began to walk away.

"And as of your sixteenth birthday you will start to manifest the powers of a Darkling," he said, following me. "One who is half demon and half human."

"A Darkling?" I sputtered, coming to a stop and glaring at him.

"You're the first one in a thousand years. Your father is concerned about how this might affect you. He had to leave the human realm over sixteen years ago and has been unable to communicate in any way since—"

I held up my hand. "Stop. Just stop, would you?"

He stopped. "I know this is a lot to grasp."

"No, not at all," I said. "I'm a half-demon princess. Sure. What's so hard to grasp about that?"

Michael was crazy. Certifiable. Maybe that's why I'd never seen him around school before—because he didn't go there at all. He was an escaped mental patient. Somebody dangerous and about to have a major psychotic break if he hadn't already had one. And for some reason I'd managed to work my way into his delusion. Just great. It was sick and twisted, and I'd feel sorry for him if I didn't feel incredibly concerned for my own safety.

He eyed me warily. "So you accept everything I've told you?"

"Demons don't exist."

"Yes, they do."

"No, they don't."

He sighed. "I'm sorry I wasn't able to explain it properly. That's why you have to come with me and see for yourself."

I backed up a step. "I'm not going anywhere with you."

"Please, Princess, your father needs to see you. You have to come with me—"

But I wasn't listening anymore. I turned and ran away from him as fast as my feet could carry me, thundering up the stairs in record time and down the street to my house where I slammed the door behind me and tried to put Michael out of my mind forever.

3

Just as I'd expected, the house was empty when I got home. I turned the lock and stood with my back against the door, trying to bring my breathing back to normal while my head throbbed with pain.

I still had the envelope he'd given me clutched in my fist.

At least I'd gotten away from him. I guess I was a faster runner than I thought. I let out a long, shaky breath and tried to relax.

I was home. I was safe. Everything was fine.

Breathe.

I went into the kitchen and saw that my mother had left me a plate of food in the fridge—vegetable lasagna and salad—and a note reminding me about the party that night.

I wasn't hungry. Not even for leftover birthday cake.

When I passed the door again, I glanced out the side window and felt my insides freeze.

Michael was in front of my house at the end of the driveway.

Just standing there.

My heartbeat, which had just calmed down to normal, picked up its pace and panic welled up inside me again.

He'd followed me home. *He knew where I lived.*

I dropped my backpack with a thud and went to the phone. I'd call 911. They'd take care of my escaped-mental-patient stalker. Just as I reached for the phone, it rang and I shrieked, nearly jumping right out of my skin.

I picked it up and held it to my ear.

"H-h-hello?" I croaked out.

"I didn't know you had a stutter," Melinda said, obviously amused. "You should probably work on that. Listen, I wanted to know if anything else happened with Chris. Since I'm your official matchmaker, I'm painfully curious."

"Melinda," I whispered. "You have to help me."

"Help you? With what?"

My hand was sweating and I cradled the phone between my ear and shoulder so I could wipe it against my jeans. "That guy from the cafeteria. He followed me home. He stopped me in the park and told me the craziest things."

"He followed you home? Are you okay?"

"I'm fine. But he's outside my house right now."

"Have you called the cops?" she asked, concern now evident in her voice.

"I was going to, but you called first."

"What did this freak tell you?"

"He said that I'm the daughter of a demon king from another dimension. And he wanted to take me to this other dimension to meet him."

"A demon king," she repeated.

"Yeah." When she didn't say anything for a moment, I prompted, "Melinda?"

"This sounds too crazy to even come from a crazy guy. Besides, the guy in the cafeteria looked like a loser, but not a *crazy* loser."

"I don't know what to do."

She paused. "You know what I think this is?"

"What?"

"I think somebody's playing a practical joke on you. It's probably Chris's friends. They know that he asked you out and they're—"

"Trying to scare me to death?" I managed. "You really think that's all this is?"

"Did he try to hurt you?"

I held the phone so tightly my fingers were numb. "No."

"And where is he now? Still outside?"

I pulled at the curtains and peeked out again. Michael was gone. I scanned what I could see of the dark street but saw nothing. "I can't see him anymore."

"Figures. Maybe Chris found out and called the guy off."

The panic was quickly stepping to the side to make way for a seething annoyance. "Well, I don't find it very funny."

"They got me once. And trust me, it wasn't funny either, but they didn't mean any harm by it." There was silence for a moment. "But call the cops if you think it'll make you feel better. It would serve them right."

I checked the driveway again. Nothing. Michael was gone. "If he was still out there, I would, but now I'll just come off as a paranoid teenager."

"You okay now?"

"I'm okay."

"Good. Now forget about the crazy loser guy. You have to tell me everything that happened with you and Chris."

So I did.

I talked to her for ten minutes about the dance—and her date and what she was planning to wear—until I felt better. After I hung up the phone, I figured I'd get started on my studying.

I was so mad that I'd allowed myself to believe Michael's stupid joke. That jerk was probably laughing right now at how gullible I was.

Other dimensions. *Sure.*

I wondered why I hadn't thought of it myself without Melinda's help, as I shakily walked through the dark and silent house and up the staircase to my bedroom. Lining the walls were framed covers of my mom's romance novels. Being married and divorced multiple times hadn't done much to change the fact that she was a hopeless romantic and she loved to talk about—and write about—being in love. My father had never been part of those conversations, though.

My eyes narrowed at the thought of my father. If I did have the chance to someday meet the man who had left her alone, I'd have several choice things to say to him, none of which was, "Nice to meet you, Daddy."

Demon king.

I was sure he was a demon, all right. But of the purely human variety.

By this time, the envelope Michael had given me was all

wrinkled up, and I threw it on my bed along with my backpack. My stomach was churning and I still had my headache.

I wondered what the point of the practical joke had been—other than just messing with me. I was supposed to read this note and then go with him. Where was he going to take me? Or would he have come clean about everything before that?

Not to mention, how did he even know that I'd never met my father before? That was inside information I didn't share with just anyone.

Strange.

On the other hand, what if the letter *was* from my father after all? I was sure he was out there somewhere in the world. When not imagining that he was dead, I would imagine that he was in jail. That's probably where he was. And now if he was writing to me . . . maybe it was to borrow some money. Maybe he had some mob bosses after him, wanting to break his kneecaps unless he came through with cold, hard cash.

Yeah, that made total sense.

I was sure he was a bad guy. What kind of person would abandon his unborn child? And leave a beautiful woman like my mom?

I frowned. What was I even thinking? The envelope wasn't from him at all. I was totally obsessing.

Just a practical joke. Right?

If that was the case, then why were my arms crossed so tightly that I couldn't even feel my hands? All over a stupid envelope?

I grabbed it off my bed and sliced it open with a finger-nail. Something heavy and loose slipped out and fell to the floor. I leaned over to pick it up and realized that it was a bracelet. A thin gold chain with one charm—a clear crystal in the shape of a teardrop. It was very pretty, actually.

With the bracelet dangling off my index finger, I pulled a folded piece of paper from the envelope. I held it in my hand for a good three minutes before unfolding it and focusing enough to read the short, precisely handwritten message:

Dearest Nikki,

As Michael has explained to you, it is imperative that I see you immediately. There is much to explain about who you are and what it means. Now that you've turned six-teen, time is of the essence. You may have trouble believing all of this, or you may have already experienced the side effects of being a Darkling—one who is half demon and half human. Please try to open your mind to this, because it is the truth. Wear the bracelet I've given you. It will help focus your power and may, with practice, make it man-ageable. Let Michael lead you to see me, I trust him implicitly. I look forward to finally meeting you after all this time.

Your father

I set the letter aside. My hands were shaking.

My father was a demon king. So that meant I was a half-demon princess—a Darkling? He ruled the . . . what had Michael called it? The Shadowlands?

The letter had talked about side effects. Well, other than a persistent headache, I hadn't experienced anything strange since I turned sixteen. So what was it? A magical headache? A demonic migraine?

I glanced at my reflection in my vanity mirror. Long, straight honey blonde hair. A scattering of annoying freckles on my nose that only went away if I took the time to use both foundation and pressed powder. Hazel-colored eyes with golden flecks. Pale lashes that required two coats of mascara to give the look of actual eyelashes.

Well, hello there, demon princess.

What a joke.

I tore the letter into itty-bitty pieces and then threw them in the toilet bowl. I flushed them away before going downstairs to take two Tylenol with a glass of milk. Stress headache. That had to be it.

Even though I'd rationalized the entire experience, I still felt shaken and tired and more than a little mad. It had been such a great day and this Michael freak had to go and ruin it for me. I couldn't even concentrate on studying, so I decided to forget about it. There would be some time in the morning to read about the doomed star-crossed lovers and try to fake my way through the test.

I was exhausted. Utterly exhausted.

At least one good thing had come out of this lousy experience, though.

I had a really nice, shiny new bracelet.

Even though my first inclination had been to flush it

down the toilet along with the pieces of the letter, I'd stopped myself. It was way too pretty to throw away.

Besides, Robert-the-jerk would probably kill me if I clogged up his plumbing. He was funny like that.

⁂   ⁂   ⁂

The next morning, I left the house early enough to walk to school the long way. I wasn't taking any chances by cutting through the park again. I'd decided to wear the bracelet, and the teardrop crystal sparkled in the sunshine. I tried to forget who'd given it to me and just enjoy it for what it was.

Besides, I figured it was probably fake and would turn my wrist green by lunch. Then I'd throw it away. It was a plan.

I turned the corner at the end of my block and my stomach sank.

"Not you again," I said, feeling my heart speed up as crazy-stalker-practical-joke guy stood blocking my way. "I'm not in the mood this morning."

Michael's hands were still shoved deeply into the pockets of his blue hoodie. In fact, he wore the exact same clothes that he had yesterday.

"Did you read it?" he asked.

I willed myself to remain calm. "Read what?"

"The letter."

"You can let it go now," I said through clenched teeth as I started walking again. "The joke's over."

"What joke?"

I glared at him. "The joke that makes you feel like you need to stalk me. It's not funny."

"I'm not stalking you."

"Could have fooled me."

He kept pace with me, since I wasn't slowing down. "Your father needs to see you immediately, Princess."

"Don't call me Princess! Would you just let it go?" I was sure that my face was now flushed, which did nothing to help the freckle situation. "Leave me alone or I'm going to tell Chris."

"Who's Chris?" he asked.

"Like you don't know. Chris Sanders? Pretty sure he outweighs you by about thirty pounds. You wouldn't stand a chance if I told him you were bothering me."

Michael's green eyes narrowed. "I wouldn't be so sure about that."

Great. The guy was stubborn as well as crazy.

With a haircut and trendier clothes, though, he'd fit in just fine at Erin Heights—and he was definitely cute enough to be one of Chris's friends. It was annoying how good-looking I found him, despite what a jerk he was being, but I pushed that aside.

"I did read the letter," I said.

"And? Are you ready to go? I can find a dimensional gateway, but it might take me a few minutes. Then we can see King Desmond."

Hold on. I stopped walking and began to feel sick to my stomach.

"What did you just call him?"

"King Desmond," he repeated.

My father's name *was* Desmond. I knew that. That was the one piece of information my mom had definitely shared with me—and which I'd never shared with anyone else.

"How do you know his name?" I asked.

"Because . . ." He looked confused. "Because he sent me here personally. I already explained this to you."

I turned my attention to the sidewalk in front of me and started moving again. "I have to go to school."

"School is meaningless right now."

"Explain that to my mother."

"Princess, please." He grabbed my arm and I tensed. He immediately let go of me. "Please stop walking for a second."

I stopped and turned to look at him. "The name is Nikki. Not Princess."

"*Nikki.*" He said it oddly, as if he wasn't certain he should be saying it at all.

I watched the air puff out in front of me with every quick exhale I made. However, when Michael breathed, there were no puffs of frozen air.

That was odd.

"I can prove to you that what I've told you is true." His brow lowered with concentration and then he looked down at his chest. "My amulet. It's not from this world."

His sweatshirt hung open and I couldn't believe he wasn't cold—the morning was just as frigid as last night. He wore a strange pendant that rested over his T-shirt—a gold chain with a large green stone, like an emerald, but I didn't think emeralds came that big. It was literally the size and shape of a flat egg. The strange stone appeared to pulse with light under the gray skies. I tilted my head to the side as I studied it.

It was the exact same color as Michael's eyes. What was it made of? I felt a sudden, overwhelming urge to touch the stone, and I reached toward him.

"Princess, don't—" Michael seemed to freeze in place as I moved closer. My fingers brushed against the softness of the worn T-shirt before lightly touching the stone itself.

ZZAAPPPP!

The painful shock shot up my arm and I jumped back from him.

"What the—?" I held my jarred hand against my chest. I felt as if I'd just stuck my finger into a light socket.

Frowning deeply, Michael took a big step away from me. "You shouldn't have done that."

"Why did it do that? Are you plugged into something electric?"

"Just—" His chest moved in and out with increased but non-frosty breathing, and he quickly zipped up his sweatshirt, pulling the hood over his dark hair. I noticed his throat working, the Adam's apple shifting as he swallowed hard. "Just don't touch me again."

I didn't particularly like the way he said it. As if I couldn't keep my hands off him.

"Your father will be angry." He stared at me, and something resembling fear replaced his previously guarded gaze.

"I don't know who he really is or why he sent you, but I don't want to see him. Feel free to tell him that."

Instead of insisting he escort me to my oh-so-important father/daughter meeting, Michael turned away and stormed off without saying another word.

My hand still stung from touching his amulet.

Not a practical joke.

Not crazy.

He knew my father's real name.

What in the world was going on?

4

I walked to school on autopilot, my thoughts in a million different places, and none of them, unfortunately, on my English test. I was definitely going to fail it. Accepting the inevitability of that was probably the best approach.

Michael was seriously freaking me out. Was it possible my real father had sent him to get me? And what was his amulet made of? Why would he be wearing something dangerous like that?

I wished that when I looked into his green eyes, I'd just see a crazy guy looking out at me. But the more I thought about it, the more I realized that all I saw was sincerity.

"Hey, Nikki!"

I looked to my left to see Chris, hanging out by the lockers with his jock buddies. The ones who I'd convinced myself were playing the practical joke on me. Of course, now I knew it wasn't a joke.

I really wished it was.

"Hey, yourself." I forced a smile to my face, trying to push away all other thoughts, and approached him. I prayed that no poppy seeds from my hastily eaten breakfast bagel were stuck in my teeth.

One of his buddies grinned. "Why don't we leave you two alone?"

The rest of the guys laughed and walked away down the hall.

I didn't know what to make of their reaction to me. Maybe I had one big poppy seed in my teeth. Maybe they were laughing about Chris asking me to the dance. Or maybe it was something completely different. Even on a good day, when somebody laughed around me and I wasn't in on the joke, I assumed that they were laughing *at* me. Sure, call me paranoid, but when you're the new kid it was true more than not.

Chris smiled at me. "You look great this morning."

I guess I looked more relaxed than I felt, but it was so good to see him—a wonderful, normal guy who made me happy just by his presence and didn't give me any problems. "You look pretty great yourself."

He leaned closer to me and kissed me. It was a morning greeting I could very easily get used to. After a moment he pulled away and his gaze moved to the right.

"Nikki, we seem to have an audience again," he said.

I turned around in Chris's arms and tensed when I saw that Michael stood about fifteen feet down the hall on the opposite side. He watched us, his face void of expression.

"Do you want something?" Chris asked.

Michael eyed him unpleasantly. "Nothing from you."

I tried to grab Chris's arm as he pulled away from me. "Chris—"

But it was too late. Chris was already moving to stand in front of Michael. They were both the same height, around six feet tall. But where Michael was all sinewy, all lean lines under those loose-fitting clothes, Chris was solid muscle under designer threads. Michael's hair was shoulder length, dark and shaggy, but Chris's was blond, recently cut, and gleaming from whatever hair products guys use to get that controlled-but-tousled look.

"Do you have a problem with me for some reason?"

Michael's attention was now fixed on me. "I'm not sure yet."

"You're not sure?" Chris repeated. "What exactly do you think you're looking at?"

Michael was looking at me so intensely that I could feel it.

"I'm looking at Nikki Donovan," he said. "I need to protect her."

I found that I couldn't stop looking at Michael. It was as if he'd captured me in his green-eyed gaze and wouldn't let go. I wanted to tell Chris what Michael had said—all the crazy things about my father that didn't seem to make any sense. But I didn't say anything. I knew I should be looking at Chris, but the only person I could see was Michael—and that haunted, protective look in his eyes.

"I suggest," Chris's voice cut through, "that you look somewhere else and leave her alone."

"And I suggest," Michael said calmly, "that you mind your own business."

I bit my bottom lip. That was definitely not a good response.

Chris's eyes narrowed. "You need to leave now."

Michael's attention finally moved from me to Chris. "I'll leave when Nikki does."

"She's not going anywhere with you if that's what you're thinking." Chris's expression was becoming less friendly with each passing moment.

Michael glared at him. "I thought I told you to mind your own business."

Chris grabbed a handful of Michael's T-shirt and pushed him up against the lockers.

"You need to leave *now*," Chris growled. "I won't tell you again."

With one hand, Chris shoved him a few feet down the hallway. Michael's cool, slightly sullen exterior had slipped a bit. Under the line of his dark hair, I could see a glitter in his eyes as he looked back at Chris. Was it anger? I wouldn't be surprised. Nobody liked being pushed around first thing in the morning in front of a growing crowd of students.

But the look in Michael's eyes as he glared at Chris made a shiver run down my spine. It was more than anger. It was the look of a predator. Then he glanced at me for a moment—at my deep frown—and his expression softened.

::Are you coming with me or not, Princess?::

I looked around. Where had that come from? It definitely wasn't my thought.

::Princess? Can you hear me?::

My eyes widened. Could I read his thoughts? Were those Michael's thoughts?

I shook my head slowly. *No, that's impossible.*

"I'm staying right here," I said, my voice shaky.

"Fine. I'm not going to force you," Michael said out loud, and it didn't sound remotely friendly. When he turned and walked away I had the insane urge to run after him, but I didn't go anywhere. I stayed frozen where I was.

Chris watched Michael move down the hall. "Yeah, just like I thought."

Michael's shoulders went rigid, but he kept walking until the door at the end of the hall clanged shut. The crowd dissipated until only Chris and I remained. The bell for first period rang.

He turned to me. "Are you okay?"

I nodded shakily.

"What a loser," he said, then he started to look concerned. "You don't already know him, do you?"

I shook my head. "Not really."

"Thought for a minute he was an ex-boyfriend of yours. All obsessed. It happens."

"Definitely not." I tried to ignore the sick churning feeling in the pit of my stomach.

"It'll be fine. He won't bother you again."

"If you say so."

"I do." He grinned after a moment. "Thought I was going

to have to fight him for a moment there—defend your honor, or something."

I forced an unsteady smile to my face. "My knight in shining armor."

"I kind of like the sound of that." He leaned over and gave me a quick kiss on the cheek. "You sure you're okay?"

"I'm fine."

When he took off for class, I pressed back against the locker door and slowly slid to the floor. I gathered my knees close to my chest and tried to breathe, before scrambling through my backpack for my bottle of water. I took two Tylenol to combat my headache.

There was only one thing on my mind then. *Michael.*

Before, when he'd followed me into the park, I'd been afraid of him. I was still afraid, but there was something else there now as well.

"I need to protect her," he'd said.

No. I didn't want to think about this. Any of it. I pushed all thoughts of Michael out of my mind and began thinking about *Romeo and Juliet.*

Romeo had been hot, dangerous, and mysterious, too. He was also totally obsessed with Juliet.

But that story hadn't ended so well.

I had everything I wanted, finally, after sixteen years of life. Other than the mountains of snow, life in Erin Heights could not be better. I was dating Chris now, who was great and brave and all defensive of me, which was nice—during his little confrontation with Michael he'd practically announced to the world we were officially seeing each other, hadn't he? I wasn't going to overthink things and chance screwing everything up.

My life was good. And I wouldn't let letter-writing absentee fathers or crazy, cute stalkers ruin it for me.

✳   ✳   ✳

After the test, which wasn't half as bad as I'd expected—after all, I had seen the movie version with Leonardo DiCaprio at least three times—the rest of the day was a blur. The buzz in school mainly concerned the formal tomorrow night. The social committee was already decorating the gymnasium to look like a winter wonderland. I took a quick peek as I passed by on my way out of the school at four o'clock, and I saw large white paper snowflakes, a ton of tinsel, and what might have been a ten-foot-tall cutout of a snowman.

There had been no sign of Michael since that morning. I figured Chris had managed to get the guy to leave me alone once and for all.

So why was that thought oddly disappointing?

I took a moment to try to hear his voice in my head, like what had happened earlier, but there was nothing. I knew I hadn't gotten that much sleep last night. It had to have been my imagination, not actual telepathy.

This was also oddly disappointing.

I touched my new bracelet. So many questions and not enough answers.

"Need a ride home?" Melinda pulled up alongside me in

her red VW Beetle. Two of her other friends, Larissa and Brittany, were also in the car. "It's freezing out there."

She was still so sure that the whole thing with Michael had been a practical joke and I hadn't tried to convince her otherwise.

I smiled at her. "Thanks, but I need the exercise. I'll be home in ten minutes."

Ten minutes because I was planning on taking my shortcut. If Michael was still around, I figured I might find him there.

"Everything okay?" Melinda asked. "You look way distracted."

I almost laughed at her major understatement. "You could say that. But I'm fine."

She didn't look convinced. "Call me later, okay?"

I promised I would and she drove away.

Currently Melinda was obsessed with beating out another girl for Winter Queen and it was a huge deal for her. I was sure our phone convo later would revolve mostly around that subject.

Since my mom and I'd moved around so much in my life I'd always had acquaintances and sometimes friends, but I'd never had a real best friend I felt like I could confide all my secrets to. Even though I felt comfortable with Melinda, I wasn't ready to tell her about Michael. Frankly, I didn't even know what I'd tell her that didn't sound crazy and paranoid.

When I crossed the bridge over the river in Hungry Hollow I noticed that Michael definitely wasn't there.

But somebody else was.

There was a big guy standing in my path, feet spread, arms crossed over his chest.

Now, when I say big, I mean big. Like huge, massive, tank-like. His hair was cropped so short he looked practically bald. He wore black jeans, big army boots, and a black sleeve-less shirt. Despite the fact that it was freezing—I'd worn my mittens, hat, and scarf today—he didn't look cold. He stood, blocking my path, with his hands on his hips.

I stopped walking when I saw him.

"I've been waiting for you," he said.

My eyes widened enough that I thought I might get frost-bite on my eyeballs. "I think you have the wrong person."

"You're Nikki Donovan, aren't you?"

I shook my head slowly as my gut began to twist with dread. "Nope. Not me. I know her, though. She should be coming by any minute."

He didn't move. "No, you're her. You can't lie to me."

I swallowed hard. "What do you want?"

"What do I want?" He tilted his head to the side. "I want to kill you, Princess."

5

A fist of panic clutched at my chest when the guy produced a knife with a big silver curved blade and moved closer to me.

I knew I had to run, but I couldn't move. I couldn't think. I couldn't even find the air to scream.

And then suddenly Michael appeared, walking down the path opposite to me as if he were simply out for a leisurely stroll, his hands in the pockets of his zipped-up sweatshirt. Just a regular guy minding his own business.

Except for his amulet. It was out and it glowed a vibrant green. He pushed the hair off his face and I realized that his eyes glowed with the same color.

His eyes were literally *glowing*.

When he was ten feet from the thug, Michael stopped walking. "Don't get any closer to the princess. Consider this your one and only warning."

The huge guy glanced over his shoulder. "Mind your own business, Shadow scum."

Shadow? What was that supposed to mean? Did they know each other?

"This *is* my business." Michael raised his right hand

and I watched with disbelief as a pulse of green light emanated from it, hitting the guy squarely in the chest. The knife flew out of his hand and he lurched to his left, crashing into the trunk of the huge, snow-covered oak tree in the dead center of the park.

"Come on!" Michael yelled, holding out his hand to me.

I wasn't sure if I was more terrified of the knife guy or what I'd just witnessed Michael do. But I grabbed on to him with my mitten-covered hand. "He was going to kill me!"

"We need to get out of here now."

Instead of taking a typical route out of the park, Michael pulled me along with him up the side of a steep hill and through a broken fence. After a few minutes, we emerged on a side street near the main downtown area. Before I could say anything else, he yanked me behind him into an alleyway.

I put my hands on my knees as I tried to bring my breathing back to normal. My head was screaming in pain now—it didn't seem to matter how many pills I took, the headache was here to stay. After a moment, I turned to look at Michael warily, a million questions bubbling to the surface.

He didn't look so good.

"What's wrong with you?" I asked.

His face had turned pasty white. There was a sheen of perspiration on his skin. The amulet wasn't glowing or even pulsing anymore. In fact, it had gone from an intensely vibrant emerald green to a dull, listless gray. Strangely enough, his eyes had lost their matching color.

He collapsed to his knees. "I'll be okay." His voice was weak. "I just . . . I just need a minute."

And then he passed out, crumpling heavily against me.

"Michael—" I crouched down and shook his shoulder. "Wake up!"

We were tucked into the alley behind a big green Dumpster belonging to a place called Dave's Diner. I could hear the guy who'd pulled a knife on me—I was sure it was him—as his army boots pounded against the pavement and stopped right at the alley.

I held my breath, clinging to Michael's unconscious form, hugging him tightly against me, too scared to move.

After what felt like an eternity, the heavy boots pounded again and soon I couldn't hear them anymore. I let out a long sigh of relief but didn't feel safe enough to move. When I finally shifted position so I could see Michael better, his eyes were still closed.

I pushed the dark hair off his forehead so I could clearly see his face. "Michael . . . please wake up."

The amulet lay heavily outside his sweatshirt. The stone was still gray, but not as colorless as it had been before.

I moved Michael to lay him down on the snow-covered ground completely, cradling his head on my lap so it wouldn't hit the hard pavement. He suddenly looked so helpless. Not like somebody who'd gone from scaring the crap out of me to saving my life.

What had he done, anyway? The green pulse. I saw it with my own two eyes. It looked like magic, but that was impossible.

I chewed my bottom lip. Maybe it wasn't so impossible.

Magic or not, there was no doubt in my mind that, based on his current state of unconsciousness, whatever he'd done had almost killed him.

He saved me.

I forced myself to be patient while he slept, sensing that he needed to regain his energy. He was breathing, though. I checked his throat to feel a pulse and it was there. I looked down at him. His eyes were closed and I stroked his dark hair, surprised at how soft it felt sliding through my fingers.

He saved me, I thought again, stunned by this revelation.

His mouth was parted a little and I still couldn't see his breath in the cold air like my own. Such a small thing seemed so incredibly odd. I moved my hand from his hair to his mouth, tracing a line along his bottom lip. I could feel his breath warm against my skin, but it didn't leave an impression in the air.

"Who are you?" I asked softly, as my touch moved from his mouth to his cheek and along the left side of his face. When he was asleep like this, I felt much more confident. I knew I wouldn't be doing this if he were awake.

I looked down at his chest where his amulet lay, and I watched as the stone became greener and greener the longer Michael slept, until it looked like it had before. What was it? I knew the amulet had to have something to do with what had happened in the park. When the emerald-like jewel had lost its color, its power, so had Michael.

I touched the chain, being careful not to touch the stone itself, but studying it closer than I had been able to before. It was very beautiful but very strange. I moved my hand until it was only an inch away from the amulet itself, in the center of Michael's firm chest. I absently noticed that his heart had begun to beat faster than before.

Quick as lightning, his hand shot out to grab my wrist, squeezing it tight enough to hurt. His eyes snapped open and they were nearly as green as they had been before his little display of . . . magic. Or whatever. When he saw me, his brows drew together and his grip on my wrist lessened slightly.

"I thought I asked you not to touch me," he said weakly.

My cheeks suddenly blazed with heat as I realized that I'd practically been groping the guy while he was unconscious.

I tried to pull away but noticed that his voice was the only thing that was currently weak. "I . . . I wanted to make sure you were still breathing."

That's all it was. I sounded convincing enough, didn't I?

He let go of me, took a moment to sit up, and then grimaced as if it caused him pain. "Are you okay, Princess?"

My eyebrows went up. "Am *I* okay? I should be asking you the same question."

He blinked slowly. "Well, are you?"

"Yeah, I'm fine." I let out a long shaky breath. "But you're going to have to tell me what's going on because I'm really freaking out here."

He winced as he slowly got to his feet. "I already told you what's going on. And we're wasting too much time. We have to get to the Shadowlands and see your father. He needs to know that somebody tried to attack you."

"Who was that guy?"

"I don't know. I've never seen him before." His jaw tensed. "You're a demon princess—the first one in a thousand years. This will attract a lot of . . . unwanted attention, now that your existence can't be hidden any longer. But I don't understand how he got here. I was the only one allowed to leave the Shadowlands. Your father was right to fear for your safety."

A shiver ran down my spine. "My father. The demon king."

"That's right."

Same story, different day. But today it sounded bigger, broader . . . and way more possible.

Too much had happened for me to sanely continue to think that nothing strange was going on anymore. Strange and, by the look of that knife, potentially deadly.

"You saved my life." My throat hurt as I said it, and when I looked up at him our eyes locked. "You saved my life back there and it nearly killed you."

His expression was firm. "You shouldn't have stayed with me. You should have gone home."

"You thought I was just going to leave you here? You were unconscious."

"I recovered."

I cleared my throat. "I know I haven't exactly been all that nice to you—"

"You don't have to be nice to me," he said firmly. "I only did what was necessary to ensure your safety, Princess."

I frowned. "Please don't call me that."

He didn't look angry or impatient with me, instead he looked concerned. "I know this is a lot to grasp. I do. And so does your father. But it doesn't make any of what I've told you less true. You're the heir to the throne of the Shadowlands. Since you're part human, you've been shielded from this knowledge and any potential danger until your sixteenth birthday."

"Happy birthday to me," I said absently.

"Your father doesn't know how your powers will manifest and he's very concerned about you. You have to come with me before it's too late."

"How my *powers* will *manifest*?" I repeated, gaping at him. "I don't really like those words."

He bent over a bit and braced a hand against the wall behind him. The green of his pendant was still duller than normal. I could tell he wasn't feeling up to full strength yet. In fact, by the strained look on his face, I was surprised he was standing. I closed the distance between us and was about to touch him, but I stopped myself.

"Are you sure you're feeling okay?" I asked.

"I'll survive." He attempted to straighten up a bit but failed. "Forget about me for a minute. Your powers . . . have you noticed anything?"

Powers? Maybe *he* was otherworldly in more ways than one, but I definitely wasn't. "Other than a persistent headache, there's been nothing out of the ordinary in my life. Well, other than you."

He actually grinned at that and looked up at me from his hunched-over position. He was even cuter when he smiled. I didn't think I'd seen that expression on him before.

"Nothing other than a headache?" he asked. "You're sure?"

"No, nothing. I'm completely normal. I mean, do I look like a Darkling to you?" I held out my arms to either side of me.

Since I'd given permission, he took a step closer and looked at me, starting at my boots and working his way up slowly. Even though I was wearing winter clothes—a thick jacket, scarf, mittens, hat—I felt like I'd just showed up in a bikini and asked him to check me out. When his gaze finally reached my face, he lingered on my mouth for a long moment before meeting my eyes again.

"Not sure." The words were a bit hoarse and he cleared his throat. "I've never seen a Darkling before."

He moved close enough to me that if I just moved my hand a little I'd be touching him. If I moved my mouth closer to his, I'd be . . .

Oh, boy.

I backed away a little. "The guy with the knife, he . . . he called you 'Shadow.' What does that mean?"

Michael's expression clouded. "It doesn't mean anything."

Then he swayed on his feet and I thought he was going to fall down again, so I reached out and grabbed his arm. He leaned fully against me for a moment, enough for me to feel the heat from his body, before he pulled away.

"I don't think your boyfriend would approve," he said. "He doesn't exactly like me."

"I'm not so sure that *I* like you," I told him, wishing I was telling the truth. "Besides, I doubt you're all that scared of Chris Sanders. You could just do that magic thing and knock him out."

"I could do worse than that," he said under his breath and then looked at me, almost guiltily. "If he ever hurt you—" He frowned hard. "Never mind. I guess I just don't like him."

Even though he'd just indirectly threatened to kick my sort-of boyfriend's butt, I felt a surge of emotion fill me. What emotion it was, I wasn't entirely sure. Michael's protective behavior was scary, but also oddly . . . *exciting.*

I was really hoping this crush I might be developing on the weirdest guy I'd ever met would leave as quickly as it had arrived. It was extremely distracting.

Michael was still hunched over a bit and had his back against the wall. His dark hair hung in his face as he studied the ground. "I'm almost fully recovered. We really must go see your father, Princess."

"It's Nikki."

He breathed out. "We still need to go, no matter what I call you."

"I want to know who you are." I took a step closer to him and was taken aback when he pressed harder against the wall.

"I told you already."

"You said my father sent you." I tried to piece it together. "So that means you know him personally. Do you work with him?"

"Something like that."

Then I had a terrible thought. "Oh, my God. You're not going to tell me that you're my half brother, are you? Because that would be gross."

The decidedly impure thoughts I'd started having about Michael would take on a whole other level of inappropriateness if that was the truth.

He looked confused for a moment, but then a glimmer lit up his eyes as he studied my expression. He raised a dark eyebrow. "Why would that be gross?"

My cheeks blazed. I was sure they had to be fire-engine red by now.

Because I think you're completely hot, I thought. But of course I didn't say it out loud. I hadn't gone that crazy—yet.

"Never mind why," I said, and then hesitated. "But are you?"

He shook his head. "Definitely not."

I let out a long sigh. "Oh, good. I mean . . . *whatever*. Doesn't really matter."

He eyed me curiously. "*Okay*."

My mind was churning. "Were those your thoughts I heard this morning in the hallway?"

"Yes," he said simply. "With a little effort we should be able to communicate that way when in close proximity . . ."

::Like now.::

I took a step back from him. "Please don't do that."

The corner of his mouth curved into a half smile, and then he glanced around the alleyway. "It's not safe here. It'll take me a minute to find a gateway. We can be in the Shadowlands and at your father's side shortly."

I held up a hand. "Whoa, there. Wait a minute. I don't remember agreeing to that."

The grin faded. "I don't understand why you're being so difficult. You want to understand what's going on, I can see that. This is the only way, and we're running out of time."

"Why are we running out of time? It's been sixteen years. What's a little more time for me to wrap my head around this whole thing?"

"Do I have to remind you that somebody tried to kill you earlier?"

I stiffened at his sudden change in demeanor. "But why can't you give me a few days to get used to all of this? My head feels like it's going to explode. I'm still trying to rationalize you telling me that my father's a demon."

"He is."

"See, that doesn't exactly make me want to see him. Demons are evil. They're . . . well, demonic. And horrible. And they live in Hell."

I waited for him to correct me on that hopefully out-dated notion.

"Well . . . they're not *all* like that," he said finally.

A shiver went down my spine. "That's not exactly comforting."

"The Shadowlands are not connected to the hierarchy of Hell in any way. And most demons are not the kind you're thinking about."

"But some of them are."

He shrugged. "I haven't met any of them personally."

My heart was pounding very fast. "Are you a demon? Is that what the guy meant when he called you a Shadow?"

"No, I'm not a demon. Princess, you don't have to be afraid. I told you I'd protect you. And your father doesn't mean you any harm, I promise. Besides, he lives in the Shadowlands, not deeper in the Underworld or Hell itself."

"Oh, that's incredibly comforting," I said, sarcasm and fear taking up equal residence in my voice.

"So are you coming with me or not?"

I crossed my arms. "Not."

He groaned with frustration. "I know I'm supposed to be patient and helpful with you, Princess, but it's becoming very difficult."

"You don't have to put up with me. If you go away and leave me alone, I won't annoy you at all."

His chest expanded as he took a long, deep breath. "I can't stay here more than two days without returning. It will damage me."

"Damage you? How?"

"I'll die."

I glanced at his amulet. Still not as green as it was when I first saw it. "You'll *die* if you don't go back? Are you serious?"

"Yes."

I clenched my hands at my sides. "Then just go back without me."

"Not going to happen."

He thought *I* was stubborn? I was getting angrier—and more confused—the longer I talked to him. I felt like hitting him. Hard. Maybe he'd leave me alone, then.

I glared up at him, breathing hard. If I was so mad at him, why did I want to grab him and kiss him? Right then. Right at that very moment.

I was definitely going crazy.

The fiery expression on his face extinguished as he seemed to realize that I wasn't going to continue to argue with him. And when I reached up to touch his face his eyes widened.

"Princess, what are you doing?"

Something about the high emotions I felt swirling wildly through me compelled me to move even closer to him, surprised at my own boldness. I wasn't like this. I didn't make the first move with guys, like, *ever*.

I pushed the dark hair off his forehead and tucked it

behind his ear. Then I moved my hand down to place it against his chest to feel how fast his heart was beating. "Why am I not supposed to touch you again?"

His throat worked as he swallowed. "Princess—"

"It's Nikki. My name is *Nikki*."

"Nikki . . ."

I slipped my hand under the zippered edge of his sweatshirt so only the thin material of his T-shirt was between us. His hand moved to my shoulder and he gripped me tightly, but not to push me away.

"I don't know who you really are, Michael, but I think you're driving me a little bit crazy."

He pressed his lips together. "Is that a good thing or a bad thing?"

"Both, I think. Definitely both."

His hand moved to cover mine, pressing it against his heart, and our gazes met and locked together. He leaned over closer until I could feel the line of his tall frame against me, until our lips were almost touching. His harsh expression softened.

"Nikki . . ."

I felt the warmth of the name against my lips, and then—

ZZAAPPPP!

My fingers absently brushed against his amulet and white-hot pain burst through my vision and coursed down my body. I staggered back from him a few steps.

I stood there trembling. What the hell?

"*That*," Michael said after a moment, his voice shaky,

"that is why you can't touch me, and it proves that I'm right. If you weren't half demon, my amulet wouldn't affect you this way."

"What is it?" I managed.

"It keeps me alive, it gives me strength, and it protects me from anything it senses might hurt me."

I shook my head. "It thinks I'm going to hurt you? *Me?*"

He looked at my mouth again. "It's a definite possibility."

This was so messed up. The one guy I wanted to kiss more than anybody I'd ever met in my entire life—even more than Chris—and I couldn't get close enough without getting electrocuted.

Oddly enough, it didn't make me want to kiss him any less. It made me want to kiss him even more.

I still couldn't accept everything he was saying. I wasn't ready. It was too much. I needed time to let it all settle.

But Michael had said he had to go back soon or he'd die. And he wasn't going back without me.

The guy was seriously melodramatic.

"I need to think," I said. "I'm going home."

"But, Princess—"

"Please." I turned to look at him. "Just give me a little time, okay?"

He didn't say anything for a moment. His jaw was clenched tightly. "As you wish, Princess."

He didn't follow me when I left the alleyway.

Which was good. I couldn't deal with this right now. Any of it. All I wanted to do was get home and plug in my straight iron.

Pretty sure my hair had gone all frizzy after that last jolt.

6

Demon.

The word echoed in my head as I jogged the rest of the way home.

Demons were horrible, ugly, evil, horned monsters who worked for Satan. They possessed people. I remembered watching *The Exorcist* a few years ago, sneaking it on the TV in my bedroom when my mom wasn't watching. I hadn't slept for a week afterward, it had scared me so much.

It didn't make any sense. It couldn't be real. And if it was . . . if I was *half* demon, what did that mean? Was I evil? Would I suddenly go all dark side and want to eat souls or something?

I had to talk to my mom. I'd demand that she tell me everything she remembered about my real father. I'd always imagined that he was some kind of monster for abandoning us, but I never would have believed he was a *literal* monster.

Then I could figure out what I was going to do next, because at that moment I had absolutely no idea.

The first thing I heard when I entered the house was

yelling. It was Robert's voice, raised as loud as I'd ever heard it during his usual temper tantrums over the last couple of months. He was yelling at my mom. Nothing new there, but it immediately made me angry.

Husband #4 was definitely in the running for the title of Biggest Jerk.

"Dammit, Susan, don't walk away from me when I'm talking to you!"

I walked into the kitchen and his back was to me, his fists tight at his sides.

"You need to calm down, Robert. Honestly, I can't reason with you when you're like this." Mom's face was flushed red, and her gaze darted over to me from where she stood by the fridge, holding a glass of water. "It's okay, honey. Just give us a minute."

"What else is new?" I asked, refraining from rolling my eyes. "Another day, another fight. It's like a really loud soap opera around here."

"Robert simply doesn't understand that when we got married I didn't sign up for having his dinner ready every night at six o'clock on the dot. When he's hungry he gets cranky."

"Call Pizza Pizza," I suggested. "Thirty minutes or it's free."

Mom smiled. "An excellent idea."

Robert looked over his shoulder at me and then back at my mother. "Are you two mocking me? That's just great."

"Robert." Mom sighed. "Calm down, would you? You're being ridiculous."

"I'm sick of this, Susan."

Her eyes narrowed. "That makes two of us. Now I suggest that you relax or you're going to have to take your temper elsewhere."

"This is *my* house."

She smiled thinly at him. "Our marriage certificate makes it half mine. Don't you forget that."

"Shut up!" He slapped her hard across the face and she gasped.

The glass she held flew out of her hand and shattered on the floor. Without a word, but with her face reddening further with obvious anger, she crouched down and immediately started picking up the broken shards, focused on her task.

My headache from hell shot through the rest of my body and pain exploded in my stomach. I closed my eyes and when I opened them, I had Robert by his arm, twisting him around to look at me.

"Never hit my mother again," I snarled at him, and then I felt something break.

It was his arm.

He yelped in pain and his expression quickly changed from rage to surprise at my unexpected strength. "Let go of me!"

I did, letting him go as if he had just burst into flames. He held his injured arm to his chest and ran from the kitchen. I heard the front door slam shut and then his car start up, tires squealing as he left the driveway.

I felt strange and out of control. My skin tingled and

my eyes began to burn. I squeezed them shut. What was wrong with me?

"Nikki, what just happened? Come back here—" I heard my mom say as I ran out of the room and up the stairs to my bedroom.

I stood against the door and tried to breathe normally, tried to will the pain wracking my body to go away. I was so mad. So unbelievably furious that anyone would treat my mom like that. The yelling was one thing, but hitting? No way. Not going to happen. Out of all of her crappy marriages over the years, the men hadn't been princes, but they hadn't been abusive either. It wasn't going to start now. I wouldn't allow it.

I breathed out. "Relax, Nikki. Relax."

I felt like if I didn't calm down something really bad would happen. Something worse than snapping Robert's arm like a twig. I moved to my vanity mirror and sat down heavily in front of it. My hair was a mess, a windblown and tangled blonde bird's nest. My face was flushed with anger. But my eyes . . .

Oh, my God. *My eyes.*

They weren't hazel anymore, they were red. Bright, glowing red, and the pupils weren't round, they were slits, like a cat's eyes. No wonder they were burning so much. Had Robert seen them change? I didn't think so. He'd only looked shocked—not scared or freaked out. Red eyes like these would definitely freak somebody out.

I squeezed my eyelids shut and forced myself to relax

until the pain began to go away, until my heart stopped pounding like crazy, until my face cooled and the tightness in my body lessened.

Slowly I opened my eyes again.

They were back to normal. But it didn't make me feel any better.

It's true, I thought, a sick feeling replacing the pain in my gut. *Michael was right. He was right about everything! I'm part demon.*

I'd wanted to kill Robert, not just hurt him. And it would have been so easy. Too easy. It felt natural.

That scared the hell out of me.

There was a knock at my door.

"Honey," Mom said. "Can I come in?"

"Y-yeah," I managed. I cleared my throat. "Come in."

The door creaked open. She had her arms crossed, a look of worry on her face. Had she seen my eyes? Did she know what I'd done? What I'd *almost* done?

"What on earth just happened in the kitchen with you and Robert?" she asked.

"I . . . I think I hurt his arm when I grabbed him." I sucked in a breath. "I didn't mean to, but he deserved it."

"I'm so sorry you had to see that," she said. "I'm sorry you had to get involved with something so unpleasant."

The fact that she wasn't grilling me on being a super-strong, red-eyed demon girl was evidence that she hadn't noticed anything too bizarre. I would have felt a sense of relief at that if I wasn't so stressed out.

"Was that the first time he hit you or is this a regular thing?" My voice was strained.

She sighed. "He's never done that before. Trust me, if he had we would have been out of here. I can forgive a lot of things, but I'm not a big fan of bruises, if you know what I mean."

"Good."

I stood up and gave her a hug. She stroked the hair back from my face and smiled. "Who knew my sixteen-year-old daughter would become my bodyguard? Have you been taking self-defense lessons?"

"It's not my fault you married somebody so fragile."

She shook her head. "So much for searching for the perfect man, huh? I don't think he exists."

"I could have told you that."

Her smile widened. "So young and so cynical already. Just like your good old mom."

I was silent for a moment. "Is that why you've been married so many times? Because you're trying to find somebody perfect? Maybe that's why you write romance novels."

"Are you trying to be my shrink? Because my messed-up love life could use some analyzing."

"What about my father?" I asked. There was no time to beat around the bush. I had to learn everything I could about him as fast as possible before something even worse happened than breaking Robert's arm.

Her mouth dropped open. "Excuse me?"

"Tell me about him. You always avoid the topic, but I really want to know. I *need* to know. Was *he* the perfect man?"

She stiffened. "Your father left me."

"I know that part already. But who was he? What did he look like? Was he nice or was he a jerk like Robert? Was there anything . . . *unusual* about him?"

Like, was he a demon from another dimension? I thought. That was unusual. Very unusual.

She shook her head. "Your father was . . . I *thought* he was the love of my life. But I was wrong. I was young when I met him. I didn't know any different."

That much I knew. My mother had been in her teens when she gave birth to me. She was only thirty-four years old now, which seemed old to me, but I knew it wasn't. Some people even mistook us for sisters.

"Your father," she continued, "took a few classes with me my first year at college. We hit it off. Went out a few times. Obviously we got a little too close too soon and I became pregnant with you. Then he left and I never saw him again. I'm sorry, Nikki, but the story isn't terribly romantic. You'll have to read one of my books if you want a happy ending."

I concentrated on everything she was saying, trying to pick out something that might help me understand. So far, nothing. "But his name was definitely Desmond."

She nodded, her face clouding over with emotion. "That's right."

"Did you love him?"

A single tear slipped down her cheek. "I did."

My heart clenched. "Where did he go?"

"I don't know." She wiped a hand across her face and looked at me sternly. For a second she didn't look beautiful, she looked tired and sad. "It was a long time ago. I've since learned that true love only exists in fiction. The sooner you accept that, Nikki, the happier you'll be in your life. Love only brings pain and disappointment."

"And men like Robert," I finished.

Her expression hardened. "Seems like it, doesn't it?"

"Are you going to leave him? Are you going to move us across the country again?"

"You'll be the first one to know what I decide, okay? I promise." She let out a long sigh. "Now, if you want dinner, there's some pasta and sauce in the kitchen. I think I'm going to my office to work for a while."

Before I could say another word, she stood and left my room.

She didn't know that my father was a demon. She couldn't possibly know.

Robert didn't come back. Not that I heard, anyway. I forced down some dinner even though I wasn't hungry and then I watched TV even though I couldn't concentrate and ended up just flipping channels. My mother's bedroom light was out by ten o'clock.

I waited until ten thirty before I quietly descended the stairs and slipped out the front door. I started walking down the street, not paying any attention to where I was going. It had started to snow again and I pulled my coat tighter around me.

I figured it would only take a minute or—

"Princess, what are you doing out? It's not safe."

—even less before he showed up.

I suppressed the smile that wanted to appear and turned to look at Michael. His dark eyebrows knitted together with concern.

"I'm curious," I said. "What's with the Van Halen T-shirt, anyway?"

He looked surprised by the question and glanced down at his shirt. "When I knew I was coming to the human realm I made sure I found some suitable clothes to wear. Isn't this okay?"

"Maybe twenty years ago. But it's fine, really." I was quiet for a moment. "Is it different here than where you're from?"

"The Shadowlands?" He glanced around the cold, dark street. "It's definitely different."

"How?"

He raised an eyebrow. "Fewer demons here."

I exhaled shakily at that. "So, are you ready to take me to see my father?" I was surprised at how confident I sounded. "Let's go now before I chicken out."

"Are you serious?"

I looked at him. "You're arguing with me?"

"No . . . of course not." He gave me one of his devastating smiles. "He'll be very pleased to see you."

"Probably not after I've had my say."

Michael eyed me for a moment. "So you're not afraid?"

I contemplated how to answer that and decided on the truth. "I'm scared beyond belief. But I don't think I can avoid it anymore."

"Did something bad happen? Did your powers manifest?"

"Still not liking those words much." I had a Technicolor flashback of what I'd forever mentally refer to as the "incident." "But, you could say that. I broke my mother's husband's arm like it was a twig."

His eyes widened at my admission. "Your strength has increased. That's to be expected, of course."

I crossed my arms tightly in front of me. "And my eyes turned red."

He put his hands on either side of my face, pushing my long hair back, and stared into my eyes. I inhaled sharply at how close we now were and it reminded me of our almost-kiss in the alleyway. "They're back to normal."

"I know that."

He didn't move away. "You're feeling better now?"

I nodded and touched his hand. "Suddenly, I'm feeling much better. Not the least bit like a demon princess."

His expression fell and he pulled away from me and started walking, abruptly putting a gap between us. What was that all about?

"Did I say something wrong?" I asked.

"No, of course not. You just reminded me who you are."

"Is that something you forget easily?" I had to hustle to keep up with his long strides.

"Unfortunately, it seems to be." He didn't look back at me. "I have to find a gateway to the Shadowlands. I need to concentrate."

"So you can just sense it?" I asked as I caught up to him.

"Yes."

"Does it have something to do with your amulet?"

"Yes," he said again.

I eyed the odd pendant lying against his closed jacket. "And you're saying that you're not a demon."

"That's right."

"You're human?"

"Not exactly."

"Then what are you?"

"I live in the Shadowlands and I help your father when he asks me to. Isn't that enough?" His shoulders went up and down as he sighed. "You're not giving me much of a chance to concentrate here. Look, I'm . . . what I am doesn't really matter."

"It matters to me."

"Why?"

I couldn't very well just come right out and say that I was starting to like him. A lot. Even though it had to be obvious, didn't it? "Just because," I said instead. "Your amulet . . . what's it made of?"

"Magic."

"*Magic*," I repeated. I already knew that, but to have it confirmed was something completely different. "Okay. So you're not a demon, you're not a human, you're this Shadow thing. But I don't know what that means. Hey, aren't you supposed to answer my questions?"

"I'm supposed to answer your questions about where we're going, take you there, and assure you that you'll be safe. I don't need to tell you about me in particular, though."

"Even if I ask really nicely?" I tried to smile at him.

::Please stop asking me. You'll find out soon enough.::

The shock of hearing his voice in my head again was enough to make me stop talking. For now.

His amulet flashed brightly once with green light and he brushed his fingers against it. "Here we are." He stopped next to a sewer grate. "Home sweet home."

"The sewer?" I said, stunned as I looked down at it. "Are you kidding me?"

"Not everything is what it seems, Princess. Remember that."

"You're not going to stop calling me Princess, are you?"

"Probably not." With a little effort, he pried open the cover, looked down into the pitch blackness below, and then back up at my stricken expression. His brow lowered. "You don't have to be afraid."

I wanted to tell him that I wasn't afraid, but that would have been a total lie. He must have seen the fear in my eyes because he moved closer to me and reached down to take my hand in his.

"It'll be okay," he said. "I'll be with you."

"Promise?"

"I promise." He glanced at the opening. "Do you want me to go first?"

I looked down at the black hole, aka the dimensional gateway. "I think that would be a good idea."

He fixed me with another one of his sexy dark-eyed gazes that made my insides turn to jelly. Even though he was standing next to a stinky sewer, wearing clothes that weren't exactly the height of current fashion, he still looked knee-weakeningly hot to me. I had a funny feeling I could be convinced to follow him just about anywhere.

"Follow me," he said. "I'll see you on the other side."

And with that, he jumped into the sewer. One moment he was standing beside me and the next he was gone.

My eyes widened and I looked down into nothing but darkness. I waited, but I didn't hear a splash. Or a scream. There was only eerie silence.

Follow me, he'd said. By jumping into a sewer? I thought he was going to climb down inside, not jump into it like it was the deep end of a swimming pool. And he wanted me to do the same thing?

Um . . . unlikely. Very unlikely.

I watched for another minute, frozen in place, waiting for something to happen.

Nothing did.

I don't know if I can do this, I thought.

He didn't telepathically project anything back to me. I guess he was out of range now.

I looked back in the direction of my house. It was around

the block and I couldn't see it anymore but I knew it was there. I could go home and crawl into my warm bed and pretend this had never happened. I didn't have to meet my father. I didn't have to do anything I didn't want to do.

But I *did* want to.

I turned back to the sewer and, without thinking twice about it, I jumped.

7

I squeezed my eyes shut and braced myself to land in a pool of unmentionable ickiness, but instead my feet touched down lightly onto something soft and springy.

I opened my eyes and looked around.

Grass. It was green grass.

I blinked and looked up to see that I was standing in a field next to a forest in the middle of the day. A moment ago it had been a cold, snowy December night, but now the sky was blue, the sun was shining, and it was very warm—especially since I was wearing my long pink winter coat and scarf, which I quickly removed.

The green stone of Michael's amulet glinted under the light.

He smiled at me.

"What?" I managed.

"You're braver than I thought you'd be."

"Brave?"

"For a second I thought I'd have to go back to get you. I'm impressed."

I squinted at him while my eyes adjusted to the sudden brightness. "Now that I think about it, I guess jumping into a sewer is a little bizarre."

Michael looked at me a moment longer, shaking his head. "I can't remember the last time somebody from the human realm visited the Shadowlands."

There was a forest ahead of us. The field of grass was spotted with wildflowers—orange, purple, and yellow dots of color across the vast field of green. A butterfly fluttered past me and I felt a warm breeze against my face. It smelled like spring.

"Wow, it's beautiful here," I said. "I'd almost forgotten what grass looks like, I've gotten so used to snow. It's like something out of a fairy tale."

He moved to stand next to me. "You think so?"

I shook my head and smiled at him. "When you said we were going to the Shadowlands, I think I was expecting something else. Hearing all that stuff about demons and Hell, I guess . . . I don't know. I'm glad I was wrong. Do we need to go into the forest? Is that where my father is?"

Michael didn't answer for a second.

"Well?" I prompted.

"This area isn't the Shadowlands itself," he said.

I frowned. "Oh. Well, where are we going, then?"

"The Shadowlands are actually behind you."

I slowly . . . *very* slowly . . . turned around and felt the blood drain from my face.

"Okay," I managed. "That's much more what I thought it would be like."

There was a castle about a half mile away from where we stood. A big one. But definitely not a Cinderella-type castle from Disney World that looked lovely and welcoming and part of the fairy-tale landscape I stood in at the moment.

The green grass and sunny skies stopped just before the castle and turned to ominous storm clouds that swirled around the castle. I could see the jagged edges of gray mountains in the distance. The castle itself consisted of sharp black spires that reached high into the dark clouds overhead. The entire structure seemed to be made of some kind of black stone. There were no windows that I could see.

Michael touched my arm. "It's really not as bad as it looks."

I swallowed hard. "Well, that's good to know. Because it looks very bad."

Dracula could totally live in that castle. Or some other monster.

Like a demon king.

Yeah, I thought. *Seems fitting. Definitely.*

I was so going to throw up.

I tore my gaze away from the castle and looked back at the forest. "I think I'd rather go in there."

Michael shook his head. "Not a good idea."

I was still trying to wrap my head around the fact that we'd just jumped into another dimension. "Why not?"

He glanced at the thick patch of trees a hundred yards away from us. "That's the faery realm."

"Seriously?" My eyes widened. "I love faeries. They're cute. They have wings."

Also, I had no idea they actually existed. I wondered if I should have brought a notebook, or even a camera, so I'd remember all of these bizarre facts. Faeries were real. Demons were real.

Okay.

I realized I was clutching Michael's arm very tightly and I loosened my grip. "Sorry."

"It's fine. I can take it." He smiled at me. "The faeries in that forest you wouldn't like so much. They're territorial. Anyone who comes onto their land is in big trouble. They can be vicious when they need to be."

I blinked. "Evil faeries?"

He studied the line of the forest with a bit of apprehension. "Not evil, exactly. Just not something you'd want to come face-to-face with if you can help it. They really don't like demons, so I don't think we should stand here for much longer."

"But I thought you said you weren't a demon?"

He met my eyes. "I'm not."

"But—" And then I shut up. Oh, right. Half-demon princess present and accounted for.

I looked at Castle Dread again. "And you're trying to tell me that there's nothing to be afraid of."

He turned completely to me. "I promised your father that I wouldn't let anything happen to you. Nothing will. Everything is going to be fine, Princess."

"And you promise to stay with me?"

A smile twitched at the corner of his mouth. "As the Princess wishes."

"The Princess definitely wishes."

His smile widened and I got that annoying little twist in my stomach again. Even here with the prospect of trekking across fairyland to go to a monster castle, Michael was making me all mushy inside.

No guy had ever made me this mushy before—not even Chris.

"Then let's go." He held out his hand to me.

I took it.

"Your hand is sweating," Michael commented, raising an eyebrow.

"That's because it's scared."

With every step we took across the field I tried to will myself to be courageous, but it was a struggle. Even though I was seeing the proof that everything Michael had told me was true, I couldn't wrap my head around it. Why didn't anybody seem to know about this place? I mean, sure people knew about Hell and the Underworld, at least in *theory*, but the fact that it was all 100 percent real? My mind boggled. Why hadn't I ever heard about the Shadowlands before?

I asked Michael the same questions.

"Humans are best kept from this sort of knowledge," he explained. "For their own good. The Shadowlands is like a buffer zone at the furthest edge of the Underworld and keeps the demon worlds separate from the human and faery realms. Nobody can pass through the Shadowlands and beyond without King Desmond's permission. That way, humans are kept safe from evil they don't even know exists."

"The Shadowlands are like the tollbooth between countries?"

He looked at me curiously. "I guess you could explain it that way."

"And my father isn't an evil demon. He's one who keeps the real evil demons away?"

That sounded like more of a gatekeeper than a king. But I guessed it was one and the same. Even though we were getting closer to the ominous-looking castle, the thought that my father wasn't a horrible, evil demon set my mind slightly at ease. *Slightly.*

Plus, holding on to Michael's hand helped, too.

It didn't take very long (unfortunately) for us to walk to the massive, black front doors. It had gotten colder as we drew closer, the green grass slowly becoming gray, uneven rock, and I put my coat back on.

"Is there a doorbell?" I asked.

Just then the doors creaked open all by themselves. I looked at them suspiciously.

"Who just did that?" I asked.

"You did," Michael said, his smile a bit out of place in such an ominous setting. "The castle recognizes you as its princess."

I swallowed hard. "Terrific. I'm like a half-demon garage door remote control."

Since my feet weren't working anymore, Michael had to pull me along with him across the threshold.

The interior was just as friendly as the exterior. As in, *not at all.* Black marble floors. No furniture. There was a huge spiraling staircase in the middle. Black, of course, since that seemed to be the sum total of the decorating palette.

I forced my feet to keep moving even though all they wanted to do was turn around and run back to where I'd come from. But I had to remember that I'd asked for this. I wanted to meet my father. I needed answers . . . to questions that had suddenly slipped right out of my mind because I was too stunned by what was going on.

"Where is everyone?" I whispered to Michael as he led me up the staircase.

"The Shadowlands isn't that populated to begin with, but recently the king has sent nearly everyone away except for a few servants."

"Why is that?"

"You'll have to ask him yourself."

I knew I wasn't the biggest social butterfly in the world, but even I couldn't imagine living in a place like this. Maybe having some friendly faces around would help, but to put up with solitude in such a dark, dreary place? That would be too much.

And Michael lived here?

I touched his arm. "It must be very lonely here."

"It can be." His eyes met mine for a second before he focused again on the stairs. "But you get used to it."

I wondered who he hung out with. Did he go to school? Were there any girls around here his age?

The thought made my stomach tighten.

No, I wouldn't be jealous. That was ridiculous. I was

already with somebody—Chris. My perfectly wonderful sort-of boyfriend at school.

I decided to focus on something else. "How many stairs are there? I can't even see the top."

"A lot. But we're almost there."

When we finished climbing the stairs—about a hundred of them—we reached a large, cavernous room that had a huge lit fireplace on one side. It was still ominous, but at least the fire gave some light and heat to the otherwise dark and dreary blackness.

Michael squeezed my hand. "You don't have to be nervous."

"Who me, nervous?" I tried to smile but failed. "I'm not."

The corner of his mouth turned up into a slight smile. "You're so lying."

"Am not." I felt a chill go down my spine. All right, so I *was* lying. Big-time. I glanced around the room. "So . . . uh . . . what happens now? Do you announce me or something? I'm just wearing jeans and a sweater. Maybe I should have picked out something nicer. I probably look terrible."

"No, you look good."

That made me smile. "Really?"

"Michael's right," a deep voice behind me said. "You're just as lovely as I expected my daughter to be."

8

I turned slowly to see a handsome man leaning against the frame of the entranceway. He was taller than Michael by a few inches and dressed casually in black pants and a dark gray button-down shirt. His hair was a few shades darker than mine and cut short. He had straight eyebrows over hazel eyes, high cheekbones, and a mouth that curved up at the side in a slight smile. I felt even more stunned than I had before.

My father looked more like me than I ever would have imagined.

And not the least bit demonic.

He took a moment to stare at me like I must have been staring at him, and then blinked and straightened his tall frame.

"Nikki," he said simply. "I'm very pleased to finally meet you."

I didn't say anything. I think I'd lost the power of speech completely. I'd figured I'd have a little more time to mentally prepare before actually seeing him, but I guessed I'd been wrong.

My father looked at Michael. "You may leave us now."

I grabbed Michael's arm before he even thought about abandoning me. After all, he'd promised to stay with me, hadn't he?

He tensed and glanced at my father.

My father's eyebrows went up a little. "I see. Well, in that case, you are more than welcome to stay for as long as my daughter requires your presence."

"Yes, Your Majesty." Michael nodded and didn't pull away from me. But his arm remained tense.

"I expected you to arrive yesterday," my father said, looking at Michael.

He cleared his throat. "I apologize for the delay."

"No, it was my fault," I managed, relieved that my voice didn't come out like a squeak. "I gave Michael a hard time because I didn't want to come at all—I didn't believe any of what he was telling me. But I'm here now."

My father glanced at my wrist. "You're wearing the bracelet I sent."

I touched it. "Yes. Thank you. It's very pretty."

"It's more than just a piece of jewelry. It will help you."

"With the half-demon thing?"

"That's right."

No one said anything else for a very long moment. Then my father cleared his throat, breaking the silence among us.

"This must all be very overwhelming for you, Nikki."

Something about the way he said it, all apologetic,

made a thick lump show up in my throat that was very hard to swallow. *Overwhelming*. Yes, this was definitely overwhelming. My brain couldn't process it all. I'd come here wanting to confront my father and ask him a million questions, but now I could barely find the words to speak. But, at least I hadn't turned and run screaming out of the castle yet. That was something.

I was using Michael as my anchor. Sure, I didn't know him very well, and the fact that he still hadn't been terribly forthcoming about who he really was didn't help. But I trusted him when he said nothing bad was going to happen.

He looked at me now with concern in his green eyes.

"You okay?" he asked quietly.

I nodded. "So far so good."

My father's expression grew more serious and his eyebrows knitted together. "I will assume that you hate me."

I shook my head. "I don't hate you."

Surprisingly, it was true. This was the man who I'd assumed I was supposed to hate for the past sixteen years, the man who'd abandoned my mother and who I wanted to give a good piece of my mind to. And yet, now that I was finally face-to-face with him, I couldn't summon up that emotion at all. Fear? Sure. But not hate.

He looked taken aback at my answer. "You don't?"

"Um . . . hating you is actually far down on the list of importance for me right now. I . . . I need some answers."

"Of course."

I finally let go of Michael's hand and he took a step back from me. I looked at him with alarm.

"It's okay, Princess," he said. "I'll be right here."

With effort, I turned my attention to my father. "So it's all true. Everything Michael has told me."

"I suppose that depends on what he's told you."

"You're a demon king? For real?"

He nodded. "Yes."

"A *demon*," I repeated as if to clarify it one more time. Maybe I'd heard wrong. Maybe it was a foreign word that meant "doctor" or "lawyer" or "construction worker."

He nodded to confirm that he was, indeed, a *demon*.

I swallowed even though my mouth was as dry as a sandbox by then. "But you look so normal to me."

"Normal is in the eye of the beholder, Nikki," he said. "I can look different should I choose to, but I felt that my human form would be best to meet you in."

I gaped at him. "Your *human* form?"

"Demons can shapeshift to either human or demon form."

I thought about my red, slitted eyes when I'd broken Robert's arm and felt a chill run down my spine at the memory. "What does your demon form look like?"

"As one brought up in the human realm, you might find it a bit . . . *unusual*." He hesitated. "However, this is how I choose to look now. You must come to realize that appearances are unimportant. I am the same man in my demon form as I am right now. The difference is merely on the surface."

I felt woozy suddenly and sucked in a quick breath of air. "I think I need to sit down."

After a moment I heard something heavy dragging across the marble floor and noticed that Michael had brought a black cushioned chair for me.

"Here you go, Princess." He smiled. "We wouldn't want you to faint."

"I'm not going to faint."

"Better safe than sorry." He stepped back again, into the shadows at the edge of the room. I wanted to ask him to stay with me, by my side, but I didn't. I could handle this. I could be brave.

But I did sit down. There was a table nearby and I dragged the chair to it. My father sat across from me and clasped his hands in front of him.

He studied me for a moment. "You look well, Nikki. I'd feared . . . that I was too late in contacting you. I worried that your Darkling would have already emerged and possibly done irreparable damage to you. Michael explained what a Darkling is?"

I nodded. "Half demon and half human."

"That's right. You're very special."

In my mind, I went over what he'd just said, trying to force myself to feel at ease, but I became more tense with every passing moment. "What damage did you expect to happen?"

His expression shadowed. "I don't know. It's been a millennium since the last Darkling lived."

I breathed out. A millennium. A thousand years. That was a long time.

"So, I guess you getting my mom pregnant wasn't planned."

"No, it wasn't planned." His jaw tightened. "However, I need you to know that I cared for your mother very much."

I felt bitter hearing that. "I'm sorry if I find that hard to believe. After all, you haven't exactly been around for sixteen years."

He didn't say anything for a moment. "I'm sure your mother must have been terribly confused."

I felt tears prick at the backs of my eyes but I refused to cry. Why did I decide to come here? I wished there had been another solution to figuring everything out. "Confused doesn't even begin to cover it. I'd go more for heartbroken, angry, pissed off, mad as hell. Those would be a little more accurate than 'confused.'"

Pain slid behind his eyes. "I never meant to hurt her. Or you."

I would have had a few more snappy comebacks to that—maybe something along the lines of 'deadbeat dads are a dime a dozen'—but all I felt was raw. Besides, this wasn't a typical father/daughter reunion. I was in the middle of another dimension in a freaking demon castle. Sarcastic comments would have to take a backseat at the moment.

"Whatever," I said instead. "Can we talk about something else?"

"No, you need to know this, Nikki. Until two days ago, I didn't even know you existed. And I thought your mother was dead."

My mouth gaped at that. I turned to look at Michael standing in the shadows, maybe to have him confirm what my father had just said. His arms were crossed and his face expressionless except for a small frown.

I turned back to my father. "You didn't know I existed?"

He shook his head. "All those years ago, I was allowed to leave the Shadowlands for one month. I'd always wanted to go to the human realm. I thought of it as just a vacation from my normal existence, but when I saw your mother . . ." He swallowed. "I fell instantly in love with her. I imagined bringing her back here to be my queen, but that wasn't going to happen."

I forced myself to breathe. "Why not?"

"I'd led her to believe I was just another student at her school, but I wanted to tell her the truth so badly. The day I was going to, I was summoned back here. One moment I was in your world, and the next I was here, unable to leave the castle."

I tried to wrap my head around what he was saying. "But . . . but couldn't you have sent a message to her?"

He pressed his lips together, his expression showing the pain he felt inside. "I tried. As soon as I could, I sent someone to find her—much like I sent Michael to find you—and when he returned I learned that Susan had been killed in a car accident. I mourned her for a very long time. I felt that if I'd been with her she might have been okay, but instead she was gone and I had no reason to try to make contact with the human realm again. I wanted to forget, or try to forget, as much as I could."

I blinked rapidly. "But she wasn't dead. I don't think she's ever been in a car accident."

"I took my scout's word as truth. However, two days ago, on your birthday, your Darkling magic became active. Since you are my daughter I could sense it, sense *you*, even between dimensions. I knew if you existed, then I had been lied to about your mother." His voice caught on the words and he took a moment to compose himself. "If I would have had any reason to believe that Susan was alive or that you existed, I never would have turned my back on you. Please believe me, Nikki."

And I did. I believed him. He wasn't lying, he wasn't just trying to make things better between us. He hadn't known that I existed. All this time when I thought he'd consciously abandoned us, he simply hadn't known.

A tear slipped down my cheek. "But . . . who would make you come back here and not let you leave?"

"My father," he said bitterly. "The time had nearly come for me to become the king of the Shadowlands. My father was near death . . ." He sighed heavily. "He had no patience for romantic notions, especially those involving a human such as your mother. The world and his duties were always black and white to him."

I looked at Michael again. He hadn't shared with me this little piece of rather important information. Then again, I hadn't exactly asked. And even if he'd told me then, when I wasn't ready to accept all of this, I'm positive I wouldn't have believed him.

"You had no idea I existed?" I knew I'd asked the question before, but it was still hard to accept.

"Not until you turned sixteen. Before that your human side was dominant. I had no sense of you at all. But now it's different." He paused. "How . . . how is your mother?"

I thought of Mom and all the trouble she'd been through raising me all by herself. The extra jobs she'd taken before she got her first novel published, and even now—she worked so hard to help me, to help us, even when there was a new husband around.

"She's good." I licked my dry lips. "She got married a couple of months ago."

His expression shifted and he looked down at the tabletop. "I'm glad to hear that she's found happiness for herself."

Happiness might be a bit of an exaggeration after that little kitchen scene earlier tonight. Also the fact that she'd been married three times before. But I decided against going into any detail about my mom's messed-up love life.

"Now," he said, "we must focus on you, Nikki. Your Darkling powers—have they appeared at all?"

I let out a shaky breath. "A little." I told him about breaking Robert's arm, although not the circumstances surrounding it. I also mentioned my red eyes.

He took it all in. "Has there been anything else?"

"Not so far."

He looked relieved. "This is very good. I was afraid that it may have come over you uncontrollably. Especially in the midst of other humans, this wouldn't be a good thing for many reasons."

I had to agree with him there. If there was a remote possibility I'd turn into something out of a horror movie, then that was definitely something I wanted to avoid. To say the least.

"So you don't think anything else will happen to me?" I asked tentatively.

"It is possible, and you must be prepared for anything. That's why I'm glad you're wearing the dragon's tear bracelet."

I looked at it and touched the teardrop-shaped crystal. "Now you're probably going to tell me that it's from a real dragon, aren't you?"

"Yes, it is. Dragons are descended from the same line as demons."

My eyes widened. "I was kidding, actually."

A small smile appeared on his lips. "But I'm not."

"Dragons," I said. "Big, fire-breathing, reptilian beasts with wings?"

"Some of them." His smile grew larger. "But don't worry. Dragons live at the other edge of the Underworld and beyond, not here. However, since you are demon royalty you would have nothing to fear—they would sense who you are and do no harm to you. In fact, they would be willing to do your bidding if you asked them nicely enough." He frowned when he saw the look of shock on my pale face. "Michael, could you get Nikki a glass of water, please? There's a pitcher on the table behind you."

A few moments later, a silver goblet appeared before me. I took it and Michael's fingers brushed against mine. I think he'd done it on purpose to remind me that he was there, nearby. His touch made a very pleasant shiver go up my arm, but when I looked up at him he'd already moved away from the table.

I drank a shaky sip of the water while I took a moment to process my information overload.

Demons, faeries, and dragons.

Oh, boy.

"This is too much," I said finally.

My father's expression grew serious again. "I know that."

"But maybe I can get used to it. I mean, I don't feel too different. If I can control things then maybe it will be okay." I took another sip of water. "Michael can help me. I can go home and come back here sometimes to visit. After time goes by I'm sure everything will start to make sense to me."

My father looked down at the table again, and then he stood up, the chair squeaking across the floor. He paced over to the entranceway and then back. His expression was tight and as he put a hand over his stomach, I noticed something was off about his posture. His expression hid something underneath that I hadn't noticed before. Pain. Physical pain.

"What's wrong?" I asked, standing up from the table. "Are you all right?"

He let out a long, shuddery breath. "No, I'm afraid I'm

not all right. I didn't want to tell you this, not yet, but there's no way around it."

I swallowed hard. "What?"

"There are reasons that it was imperative for Michael to bring you here as soon as possible. Part of it was to tell you who you are and what it all means, but there's more to it, Nikki. A great deal more. I'm so very sorry that I don't have more time to help you adjust to this vast amount of information you've been asked to accept. You've been very brave so far, I'm proud of you."

Michael went to my father's side. "Are you okay, Your Majesty? Should I get Elizabeth?"

My father tensed again and held his hand tighter against his stomach. "Not yet. It will pass."

I felt a rush of concern come over me. "Are you sick?"

He raised his head enough to look at me and there was now a light sheen of perspiration on his face. "Yes, I am. It's come over me only in the last couple of weeks. I'm having the same symptoms my father had before his death. I'm afraid I don't have much time left."

My breath left me in a rush. "You're dying?"

He nodded. "I'm functional for now, but the pain comes upon me quickly. Today I'm feeling well enough to see you here. But I know there isn't much time. A few days. A week at the most."

I tried not to cry, but I knew it was too late to stop a few big, fat tears from escaping. I watched as Michael helped him back over to the chair. "Isn't there anything that can be done?"

"No, I'm afraid not. It's unexpected. I'm still young, so I don't know why my time has come so soon. But, so be it. I have no choice but to accept my fate. However, I must use what time I have left to ensure that someone suitable will take over my throne. Someone who can rule the Shadowlands."

I wiped my face. "Michael told me that this place keeps all the bad stuff from the Underworld and Hell from coming to where I live."

"That's right. A long time ago, the Shadowlands was a place of chaos. A few demons who then lived deeper in the Underworld knew that something had to change if the human and faery realms were to be saved from destruction. They took over this land and built this castle."

"This unbelievably scary castle." My voice shook as I said it.

The pain was now gone from his face and he smiled at me. "Trust me, I wasn't consulted on the architecture. It was well before my time. But there is a reason for everything. The stone the castle is built with is infused with magic that both senses the royal line's power and helps to hold back the evil that exists beyond it. No creature, be it demon or any other, can pass without the kingdom's permission."

"Without *your* permission, you mean," I said.

"That's right. And that's one of the reasons I'm not able to leave. I can't even go outside. I haven't seen the daylight in over sixteen years."

My heart dropped at that. "How terrible."

"It's necessary, and I accept it. I take my responsibility

very seriously, and I expect anyone who takes the throne to do the same. Which leads me to the real reason it was so very urgent for me to speak to you personally, Nikki." He took a deep breath in and let it out slowly. "As my only heir, when I die, you will automatically become queen. You will be summoned here from wherever you are at that moment and shall be unable to leave the castle from that day forward."

I gaped at him. "You can't be serious."

"I'm afraid so."

I shook my head, my eyes going wider with every passing second. "No, that's impossible. I don't want to be queen. I don't want to live here." I was starting to hyperventilate at the very idea that I had no choice in this. I was used to people telling me what I had to do—my mom, Melinda, even Michael, now—but that was nothing compared to this. "I'm so, so sorry that you're dying, but I can't live here. I don't want to be a demon. I don't want any of this."

I felt Michael touch my arm and my first thought was to push him away, but instead I grabbed hold of him and hugged him tightly, pressing my face against his chest. He held his hand over his amulet so I could avoid getting zapped. He didn't say anything, but I felt him stroke my hair, trying to soothe me.

It worked, but it took a minute. When I'd composed myself, I turned again to my father, who looked incredibly distressed by this entire conversation. It obviously wasn't any easier on him than it was on me.

That helped. A little.

"Nikki," my father began.

"Please," I said, and I could hear the desperation in my voice. "There has to be another way."

"There is." His smile held but it was sad. "But first I wanted to see how you felt about the situation. Now I have."

He pulled out a chain from underneath his shirt. It was a gold chain, thinner than the one Michael wore, and on the end of it was a dark red glass bottle no bigger than my thumb. He pulled the chain over his head and handed it to me.

I took it from him and, looking down at it, I realized the bottle wasn't red at all, but the liquid inside of it was. "What is this?"

"A magic potion. For you."

9

I frowned at him so deeply it hurt. "A *magic* potion?"

He nodded. "It will remove any trace of demon from you and the kingdom will no longer recognize you as my heir."

My eyes were wide. "I don't understand."

"This is the only way your life can remain normal and untouched by all of this. Drink the potion and you will become completely human. You won't have to deal with the complications of being a Darkling. As I said, I don't truly know how your powers will fully manifest and that worries me greatly."

"You and me both," I managed.

"Also, if you don't want to accept the responsibility of taking the throne when I die, this is the only way to avoid that. By drinking this you will be safe in all ways."

The gold chain hung off my hand and I looked at the bottle. It felt cool against my sweaty palm. My other hand, I suddenly realized, was clutching Michael's wrist very tightly.

"I can't believe it's that easy," I said.

"It is." My father hesitated. "However, there is a side

effect of the potion that you should be aware of. Once taken, your memories of being half demon, as well as of your trip here to the Shadowlands, will fade away."

I looked at Michael and then back to my father. "You mean I'd forget about Michael, too?"

My father's brow knitted. "Michael, I think this is a good time for you to fetch Elizabeth for me. Please tell her that Nikki has arrived."

Michael cleared his throat and disengaged his hand from mine. "Yes, Your Majesty."

I watched Michael quickly leave the room without a backward glance. "He sure follows orders well here, doesn't he?"

"Servants are required to follow the orders of their master."

The room went very silent, except for the sound of the fireplace crackling and my heart fluttering like a trapped bird.

"I don't think I heard you right," I began. "Did you just say that Michael is a *servant*?"

"Yes, of course. In fact, when I sent him to the human realm, he was specifically assigned to be *your* servant." He frowned. "Didn't he tell you that?"

I made a beeline for that goblet of water again and took a shaky sip before answering. "No, I didn't know that."

"He should have told you. It is unacceptable that he didn't. Shadows are servants to demonkind."

My head was spinning. A servant. Michael was a *servant*? "What is a Shadow?"

"The Shadowlands were once home to beings called Shadows. They were a part of the chaos that threatened the worlds beyond before the demons brought order here again. The Shadows that remained afterward were enslaved to us."

I felt stunned. "So you're saying he's a . . . a slave?"

My father looked confused by my stuttering reaction to this news. "We treat our Shadows very well and give them many freedoms, but yes. If it wasn't for us they would have been completely destroyed. Michael has been particularly helpful to me over the years."

"He lives here?"

"Yes, he was brought to the castle as a child—he is unaffected by the unavoidable solitude this place brings with it. Since he is around your age, I thought him best to travel to the human realm to bring you to see me. He's been very loyal to me, and because of this I've given him certain privileges that most Shadows would never be allowed. But . . ." He looked at me sharply. "Michael is not boyfriend material, if that's what you're thinking."

My face flushed. *"Boyfriend material?"*

"Even if he wasn't a Shadow . . . you are a princess, and therefore high above a mere servant."

"I'm starting to figure out why he didn't want to tell me what he really was," I said icily.

My father's expression grew more severe. "You asked Michael a direct question and he refused to answer?"

"No. Please, forget it."

"I recognize the signs, Nikki, and it worries me."

"The signs?"

"He doesn't look at you as I'd expect a servant to look at a princess. I fear that he's forgotten his place. I'll have to speak with him."

I couldn't believe this. Why hadn't Michael just told me? Because he was embarrassed? Ashamed of what he was?

"Michael saved my life," I said, for lack of anything else to say.

He stiffened. "What do you mean?"

"There was a guy with a knife earlier when I was walking home from school. He tried to kill me and Michael saved me. That . . . that amulet he wears—he was able to blast the guy away like he was nothing."

It took my father a moment to say anything to that. "Why didn't he mention this to me? Shadows aren't permitted to harness their powers, especially not in the human realm. It's too dangerous." He paced the room for a moment. "But if he did it to save you then I suppose this indiscretion can be forgiven." He turned to look at me again. "Was this attacker a human?"

"He looked human, but I think he was a demon. He called me Princess."

His expression shadowed. "I don't know how this is possible. Michael is the only one that I authorized to travel to the human realm. How would this assassin even know of your existence?"

I shrugged. "He could have slipped through."

"It must be because my powers are weakened by my illness. It's the only explanation I can think of." My father shook his head gravely. "You're okay, though?"

I was too focused on these newfound revelations about Michael to obsess any more about the big guy with the knife. "I survived."

"I'm very glad." He didn't say anything for a moment. And then, "Has Michael told you anything else about himself?"

"Not much." I swallowed. "But, he did say that if he didn't return here in a couple of days he'd die. Is that true?"

My father stood up and walked toward the fire. The light illuminated his stern, handsome features. "The green stone amulet he wears is made from what was once a large deposit here in the Shadowlands back when his kind ruled. They drew their power from it."

"Do all Shadows have green eyes?" I asked.

He looked at me. "Yes, they do."

"When he blasted the guy, the amulet kind of went dull and so did the color of his eyes."

"He was weakened from using his abilities in the human realm."

"But he recovered. Kind of like recharging his battery."

He nodded. "Yes, it is much like that. Michael needs his amulet to sustain his life force. In order to take the land, the demons had to destroy the deposit and clear most of it away. But since Shadows need it for survival, they were each given a small piece of it that they could wear on the outside of their clothing at all times. To keep the energy charged, Michael must remain in the Shadowlands or the Underworld, or else he will steadily weaken."

I tried to add this new information to my already full

brain. On the bright side, my headache from earlier hadn't shown up ever since the incident with Robert. "I don't understand why the demons had to take the land at all. Why couldn't they share it with the Shadows?"

My father's harsh expression softened with a small smile. "You are asking me to condense a millennium of history into a few minutes. Shadows are . . . very stubborn, difficult to control, and as you saw by what Michael did to your assailant, they are also very powerful when they have the chance to be. They are unpredictable by nature. When presented with the option of joining us, the Shadow king declined. Rather rudely, from what I understand. Unfortunately, they left us with no other choice but to use force." He paused for a moment. "Michael is a direct descendant of that king, so he does come by his insolence naturally."

I sucked in a breath of air and clutched the side of the table tightly. "So he's actually a prince?"

"No." He shook his head. "Michael is your servant. And neither he nor you should ever forget that."

I heard something at the entranceway and looked over. Michael had reentered the room in time to hear the last thing my father had said. His expression looked stricken.

"Michael," my father said, "why didn't you tell Nikki who you really are?"

His gaze was now firmly fixed on the floor. "I should have, Your Majesty."

"Please tell her now."

I could barely breathe. Why was my father making him do this?

Then Michael glanced at me and our eyes met. He looked ashamed—of who he was or of how he had kept the truth from me, I didn't know—and it made my heart twist sharply.

"I am your servant, Princess." He choked out the words. "And it was wrong of me to keep this from you. I'm very sorry."

That's why he called me Princess instead of Nikki. It was a term of respect. He'd been assigned to find me, tell me about who I was, and keep me safe. He didn't tell me who he was—he was vague and avoided the question—because he didn't want me to know the truth.

But now I knew.

"Michael, you can wait downstairs until Nikki is ready to go home," my father said sternly. "Thank you."

Michael turned and left the room.

I felt sick. He'd been completely humiliated. I wanted to hate my father for what had just happened, but when I looked at him he simply looked back at me curiously, as if he couldn't understand why I was so upset.

Servants were a normal daily thing for him here, and what he'd done hadn't been cruel or unusual for him. But not for me. Not like that. And not to Michael.

"What is it, Nikki?" he asked softly. "Why are you upset?"

Before I could say anything, somebody else walked into the room. It was a beautiful woman with long blonde hair, flawless translucent skin, and a wide, friendly smile.

For some reason, my already aching heart dropped a

little more. *The queen.* Had to be. My father may have felt badly about leaving my mother all those years ago, but that didn't mean that he hadn't moved on.

"My goodness," she said. "What did you say to Michael? He looked very distressed."

"He'll be fine," my father said. "Please, Elizabeth, come and meet Nikki."

She didn't take her attention off me as she approached and reached out to clasp my hand in hers. "Nikki," she said, beaming at me, "I'm so thrilled to meet you. I'm Desmond's sister, Elizabeth."

I raised my eyebrows with surprise at that introduction. "You're my *aunt.* So you're *not* married to my father?"

She smiled a bit wider. "Well, that would be rather inappropriate, wouldn't it?" Then her smile faded a bit. "You also look rather distressed. This is all horribly over-whelming for you, isn't it?"

"You could say that."

She touched my shoulder. "I know. Believe me, I know. This would be surprising news—to find out your Darkling nature—on a good day. Let alone with everything else that's happening here. . . ." Her eyes grew misty and she glanced over her shoulder. "Are you feeling all right, Desmond?"

He'd moved to the table and leaned against it, a hand to his stomach again. "Well enough."

Even I could tell he was lying. He was feeling pain again and, despite what had happened with Michael, concern for him welled up inside me.

Elizabeth shook her head and then went to the long black table. She poured a goblet of water from the pitcher there and brought it to him.

"Drink this," she said.

He lifted it to his lips and drank.

She glanced at me. "You do know that your father is gravely ill?"

My throat thickened and I nodded.

Her attention moved to the vial I still held in my hand. "You've given her the potion, Desmond?"

"I have."

My head still swam from all the information I'd received. Meeting my aunt only added to it. "So if I take the potion . . . when my father . . . when he . . ." I swallowed, not wanting to finish that sentence. "Who will take over the throne?"

Elizabeth helped my father into the chair and stroked the hair back from his face. His skin had gone very pale.

"Elizabeth and I have already discussed this, Nikki," my father said weakly. "She's consented to take the throne. After you, she's next in line."

"So that means . . . ," I began. "That . . . that you won't be able to leave here either? That you'll be stuck here in this castle?"

"Don't worry about me. I'll manage. Although, I may consider redecorating." Elizabeth gave me a small smile. "Truly, Nikki, it's the best solution in this unfortunate matter. You shouldn't have to deal with this burden at your age. Especially only learning about it now."

When my father died, Elizabeth would be trapped here without being allowed to leave, and she was doing it of her own free will.

"I'm sorry," I said.

"Don't be. I only wish I could have met you before all of this. I would have loved the chance to get to know you better."

I clutched the vial tightly in my hand and thought how when I drank its contents I'd forget all of this. I'd forget my father, and Elizabeth . . . and Michael. I hadn't known any of them a couple of days ago and now it actually hurt to think that I wouldn't be able to see them again.

But it was the only way.

My father let out a small groan of pain. And then a larger one as he stood up, then doubled over and clutched the side of the table.

"Desmond." Elizabeth grabbed his shoulders. "Are you all right?"

"No . . ." He gritted his teeth. "I need to go back to my room. I . . . I feel poorly. Very poorly."

And then he yelled out. The sound of his pain cut right through me like an icy wind.

I ran to his side. "Dad—"

"No, get away." His voice came out loud and gravelly. "Please, Nikki. Don't come any closer."

I heard a ripping sound and watched with horror as two large, black, leathery wings unfurled from his back. His hands went out to his sides and long, sharp claws emerged from the tips of his fingers.

I took a step back and covered my mouth with my hand.

He straightened up and looked at me. His eyes were red with catlike slits and appeared to glow in the semi-darkness of the room. There were horns—big, black, curved horns—protruding from the sides of his head. His face had grown unrecognizable, sharper, more pointed, his skin now black as coal. I got a glimpse of his teeth, which were now pointed and as sharp as razors.

He covered his stomach with a clawed hand—his chest had grown larger and muscular enough to burst the buttons on his gray shirt—and he convulsed. Even in demon form he was still in terrible pain.

"Nikki," he said in that strange, demonic voice, "I'm sorry. I didn't want you to see me like this and be afraid."

I believe my answer to that may have been a short, terrified scream. I'm not entirely positive.

He gasped for breath. "Drink the potion and forget about all of this. It's for the best."

His now-sharp jaw clenched and with a last look at me, the demon king turned and quickly left the room.

10

I stood in place shaking from head to foot.

My father was a demon.

A monster with big, black, batlike wings and sharp teeth like something out of a nightmare.

"No," I said out loud, shaking my head, even though I'd now seen it with my own eyes. It was true. There was no denying it anymore. I started to cry. I couldn't hold it in. My chest heaved with sobs.

I felt a warm hand on my back and I jumped, spinning around. It was Elizabeth. I scrambled back from her. She was a demon, too, and she would look like my father in her demon form. This human form—it wasn't real. It was just a lie. She was evil. Demonic.

"Nikki." Her eyes were glossy. "Please, don't be afraid. I know this is difficult for you, but please just try to calm down."

I looked over at the entranceway. Where was Michael? He'd said he'd stay by my side and not leave me, and now he was gone. Why? He'd promised that nobody was going to hurt me.

And nobody had. Nobody had hurt me.

I forced myself to breathe normally and I looked at Elizabeth—really *looked* at her. She didn't look evil or demonic. She looked concerned. For me. She'd backed away after my reaction to her to give me some space.

"I'm not going to hurt you," she assured me. "Everything will be fine."

It took me another couple of minutes before I felt anywhere close to fine, and even then I still felt jumpy.

"What happened?" I asked shakily. "Wh-why did he change like that?"

She took in a deep breath. "He's in a great deal of pain. It is just as it was with my father when he was near the end. In demon form we're able to handle pain better. It doesn't make it go away but it becomes more manageable. A human body is more aesthetically pleasing, but it makes us very fragile. Right now, Desmond can't control the shift. When he experiences intense pain, he simply turns to demon form. I know he didn't want to scare you, Nikki. It's the last thing he wanted."

I looked over at the entranceway. "Is he going to be okay?"

But that sounded stupid. He wasn't going to be okay. He was going to die.

"He'll be fine in a bit. We must leave him alone and let him recover enough to change form again." She patted my cheek. "Honestly, I think the best thing for you would be to let Michael take you home. You should probably drink the potion, too, and in minutes all of this will have faded away."

I looked at the potion bottle again. "Okay. I'm going to drink it." I put the chain over my head and let the vial fall against my chest. "But I'm going to wait until tomorrow, though. I . . . I still need to think about some things."

I wasn't ready to forget. Not this quickly. I'd have plenty of time tomorrow when I was back in my normal life. It could wait until then.

"I understand. But don't wait too long. It's dangerous to wait now that you're sixteen."

My eyebrows went up at that and I shifted my focus from the entranceway of the dark, cavernous room to my aunt. "Dangerous?"

She nodded gravely. "I'm sure Desmond didn't go into specific details, but there's a very good reason why there hasn't been a Darkling in a thousand years. You've been very lucky that you haven't experienced any serious consequences."

I looked questioningly at her. "What are you talking about?"

She wrung her hands together and walked over to the table, before turning back to me. Her beautiful face was tense and worried. "Desmond had me look into the history of Darklings when he first began to sense you, and I found out some things. Things I didn't want to burden him with in his current condition."

"What kinds of things?"

She didn't speak for a moment. "No Darkling has ever lived past their eighteenth year. It's the human/demon mix. It's unstable. Those who have lived that long refrained from using any of their powers at all. It's the only way."

"You mean, if I don't take the potion and become completely human then I'm going to die?" I managed.

She pressed her lips together. "But you have the potion. You will take it, and you will forget about all of this."

"But . . . but my father said that I was the heir. That if he died then I would become queen. He didn't say anything about this."

"That's because he doesn't know." She sighed. "If there was another way, believe me, I'd want to learn what it is. I don't want to be queen, you know. I don't want to never be able to leave this place, but it has to be done." She touched my shoulder tentatively. "Take the rest of the night and let it all sink in, if you wish. But tomorrow morning, drink the potion. Forget about all of this and live a happy, normal life, Nikki."

I nodded shakily. "Okay."

"But please remember one very important thing."

"What's that?"

"In the meantime, don't allow your powers to manifest. At all. They're triggered by extreme emotions. Stress, anger, fear . . . I know you've had your share of all of that today, and I'm worried about you. Do you understand?"

I nodded again. "I understand."

"Good." She rubbed a tear away from my cheek with her thumb. "I will take care of your father, I promise. I'll make his last days as comfortable as possible. I know he was so happy to find out that you existed. And he was so happy to get the chance to meet you before the end. Please know that even in his demon form, your father cares about you and would never wish you harm in any way."

I blinked back more tears. "I'm glad I met him, too. I just wish I had more time."

"Me, too."

I hugged her and she smelled like warm jasmine. I felt something press against my collarbone and looked down.

"You have a vial, too?" I asked, glancing at the small blue bottle she wore around her neck on a chain.

She touched it lightly. "It's perfume—a gift from my *inamorato* . . . or what you might call my 'boyfriend.'" Her expression turned forlorn and wistful. "I'm hoping he'll want to visit me when I'm unable to leave this castle."

She led me out of the room and down the staircase to where Michael was waiting, his attention firmly fixed on the floor.

"Good-bye, Nikki. Be well." With a last squeeze of my hand, Elizabeth left to go deeper into the castle.

The doors opened up to let me out.

Michael didn't say anything. He simply walked outside. He led me over the gray stones that slowly turned to green grass. Where the dark, stormy skies above cleared away to beautiful blue. Where the forest leading into the faery realm stood before us, looking very innocent and not like the home of unfriendly, territorial faeries.

My head ached with everything I had learned swirling around inside. Seeing my father turn demon. Learning that he was going to die. Learning that I would die if I didn't drink the potion. Meeting Elizabeth. Learning that her fate was to never leave the castle again. Knowing I'd forget all of this as soon as I drank the potion.

I sucked in a breath and it sounded like a sob. "Why didn't you tell me?"

Michael looked over his shoulder at me. "What part?"

"All of it. About my father's health. About the dangers of being a Darkling. About all of that."

"I told you what I was supposed to tell you, Princess. I answered your questions."

I felt angry then. At him, at everything. "No, you didn't. I asked you to tell me who you were but you didn't say anything. I wish you would have told me the truth."

He shoved his hands into the pockets of his sweatshirt and kept trudging along toward a shimmering patch of light about fifty feet ahead of us—the gateway back to the human realm.

"I should have told you," he said. "I know that."

"Yeah, you should have."

"Well, now you know. I'm a servant." He said it so bitterly and his eyes were still on the path ahead of him. He hadn't looked me directly in the eyes since we were in the castle. "You're a princess and I'm your servant. See? I can say it. It's not even that bad, actually."

"Michael—"

"Princess, please. Let me take you home. It doesn't matter anyway. None of this matters. When you drink the potion you'll forget all about me and everything else." He'd reached the gateway. "No sewer this time. Not as traumatic, I promise."

I looked at the gateway. It was about the size of a regular door, but with rounded edges; a swirling kaleidoscope of color, but I could still see through it to the other side as if it were only a light film.

"Wait a minute—"

::Follow me, Princess:: He didn't say it out loud this time.

I bit my lip. *Telepathy*. I could hear him because I was a demon princess and he was the servant my father had assigned to me.

Right behind you, I thought telepathically, wondering if he could hear me as clearly as I could hear him.

Without another word or a glance at me, he walked directly through the gateway and disappeared.

I looked back over my shoulder at the castle in the distance. That scary castle I'd been so afraid to approach. And there was no doubt—it *was* scary and intimidating and so very strange. Everything about this had been unbelievable. But it was all true.

My eyes filled up, thinking I'd never see my father again. I'd wanted to hate him, I'd tried to hate him, but I couldn't. He was a good man. His demon form had scared me, but he'd said earlier that he was the same person underneath. That appearances meant nothing.

Now I believed it.

Good-bye, Dad, I thought as a tear slipped down my cheek.

And then I walked through the gateway. My stomach lurched a bit and I had a moment of vertigo, but with the next step I was on the street where I lived. Michael stood there with his arms crossed as he waited for me.

"Come on," he said. "I'll walk you to your house."

I shifted my focus to Michael. "Can I ask you a question?"

"Of course."

"What do you do for fun in the Shadowlands?"

"Fun?"

I shrugged. "Here we go to the movies or the mall or just hang out. Or go to dances like Winter Formal tomorrow night at school."

"We don't have anything like that." He frowned. "There are lots of books, which is how I learned all about the human realm. I . . . I hang out with some of the other . . . servants . . . who live at the castle. They're okay."

"Anybody your age?"

He shook his head. "Not really."

I chewed my bottom lip. "Do you have a girlfriend?"

"No." There was silence then for a moment. "We're here. I guess I'll say good-bye now."

We'd reached my house. I could tell by the big maple tree at the bottom of the front lawn.

"What did you think would happen if you told me the truth about who you really are?" I asked.

"It doesn't matter anymore."

"It does matter. Did you think I'd look down on you?"

He pressed his lips together and was apparently finding

the ground an extremely interesting thing to look at. "Something like that."

"Well, you were wrong."

He finally raised his gaze to mine. "But your father said—"

"Forget about what my father said. He has a seriously outdated view of the world, but that's probably because he lives in a different one." I sighed. "Look, if this could be any other way I wouldn't take the potion at all. I don't want to forget about you. I don't want to forget about any of this."

"You have to drink it."

"I know that, but it doesn't mean I want to."

He let out a breath, but I still couldn't see it in the cold air. It had to have something to do with his amulet controlling his life force. Even in the darkness it pulsed with a soft green light over his sweatshirt.

"You can get back to your normal life with your . . . your boyfriend, *Chris*." Michael said his name unpleasantly. "I'm sure you'll be glad when all of this is over."

"He's not really my boyfriend," I admitted.

That raised his eyebrows. "But I thought you said—"

"I'm just going to the dance with him."

"I saw him kiss you in the hallway." He didn't sound happy about it. "And yesterday, too."

I thought back to Chris's hallway smooch. Had that honestly only been earlier today? It seemed like a lifetime ago.

"He's not that great a kisser," I said. "But don't tell anyone."

"I definitely won't." He glanced back at the street.

"Look, I really need to go now. Your father will wonder what's taking me so long."

"I think you worry about him too much." I walked right up to him and he glanced at me warily. I held out my hand. "Thank you for all your help, Michael."

He took my hand in his and we stood like that, silent, for a moment, and then, "Good-bye, Princess."

I just looked at him.

After a few more moments had gone by he raised his green-eyed gaze to mine. "You're not going inside."

"Not yet."

"And you're not letting go of my hand."

"I know."

He swallowed. "I can't leave until I know you're safe."

He looked away, pushing the dark hair across his forehead as if trying to hide his face from me. I reached up to push it to the side so I could see him.

"Princess . . . ," he began.

I'd sort of gotten used to him calling me that. I didn't even correct him anymore. "Uh-huh?"

"You need to go now."

I knew he was right. I should be going inside—or rather, sneaking in would be better. A quick glance at my watch told me it was nearly one o'clock in the morning. Mom would kill me if she found out I was gone this late.

"I need you to do something for me first."

He raised his eyes to mine. "What?"

"Can I borrow your sweatshirt for a second?"

Even though I was already wearing a winter coat, he

didn't hesitate to strip his own meager protection from the cold off his back and hand it to me.

"Thanks," I said.

"What do you need it for?"

"Protection," I said. "I don't want to get electrocuted again."

He looked confused. "Why would you be worried about something like that?"

"I just worry." I balled the sweatshirt up in my hands and pressed it against his chest and over the green stone of his amulet. This also pushed him back up against the tree.

His frown deepened. "What are you doing?"

"This." I leaned closer, went up on my tiptoes, and kissed him. He seemed to resist for a moment, perhaps surprised by what I was doing, but then he relaxed and kissed me back. Hard. His hands moved down to clutch my arms and pull me closer as the kiss deepened and went on and on.

"Just like I thought," I said as I brushed my lips against his again.

"What?" His voice was raspy.

"Way better than Chris Sanders. Like, there isn't even a comparison, really." I grinned and kissed him again. "I want you to know that I don't give a crap whether you're a servant or not. Remember that."

"Then I guess I don't care if you're a princess," he said against my lips.

"I don't want to drink the potion," I said, my heart clenching at the thought.

His expression darkened. "You have to."

I had to do a lot of things I didn't want to do, didn't I? "I know. But I'm going to wait until tomorrow."

"Then wait."

"I want to see you again. Promise me that you'll come back."

"I promise," he whispered.

I kissed him again, and hugged him against me. "So this is good night, not good-bye. Not yet, okay?"

He nodded. "Good night, not good-bye."

After another kiss, I handed him back his sweatshirt. Then I ran to my front door and disappeared inside.

11

The first thing I did when I woke up the next morning was look in the mirror to see if there was some sign of demon in me. But there was nothing. Other than looking exhausted from barely sleeping, I looked the same as I always had. Freckles and all.

"Nikki," my mother called out to me over her coffee and toast and the entertainment section of the newspaper. "Come have some breakfast."

I stopped at the table and looked at her—really *looked* at her for the first time in a long time. She wore her pink fuzzy housecoat and her long dark hair draped over her left shoulder.

How must it have felt to have the man you thought you were in love with just disappear without a trace, without even a good-bye first?

I wanted to tell her everything, but I knew I couldn't. She wouldn't believe me, for one thing. She'd probably send me to the nearest shrink. And even if I could convince her it was all true, could I really tell her that the love of her life hadn't wanted to leave her in the first place? And that now he was dying? It would only bring her more pain. It was best to say nothing at all.

"Is there something wrong?" she asked at my prolonged silence.

I shook my head.

"I think I know what it is," she said, putting down her cup. "It's the dance tonight, isn't it?"

The dance. Right. I'd nearly forgotten about that. "You guessed it."

"You've barely told me anything at all about it. Are you going?"

"I . . . I don't know." I adjusted my backpack and glanced at the clock. I was already running late for school since I'd slept right through my alarm. "I was invited to go. This guy named Chris asked me. But I don't have anything to wear. I haven't had a chance to go to the mall."

She smiled at me. "If that's the problem then I suppose I could let you borrow my lavender dress."

Normally, I think borrowing your mother's clothes wouldn't be so cool, but the thing was—my mom had really great clothes. Clothes that I'd actually consider buying for myself if I had any money. And I knew the dress she was talking about. It was a designer dress—Versace—that she'd bought to go to a writers' banquet a few months ago. When she got it I remember running my hands over the beautiful silky fabric and wishing I'd have the chance to wear something like it someday.

"Thanks, Mom." I went over to her and hugged her harder than she probably expected.

She looked up at me curiously. "Are you sure nothing's wrong, honey?"

I nodded again. "Where's Robert? Did he come home last night?"

"No, he's . . . he's staying with a friend for a while." She took a sip of her coffee. "I think it's probably best. It'll give me some time to think about things."

Time. It was something I needed, too. I needed to think about the potion, about Michael, about everything. And I guessed school was as good a place as any to do some thinking.

Classes that morning were a blur. I remember being asked a question by my geography teacher and I just looked at her blankly. I wasn't even embarrassed that I didn't know the answer.

I wore the vial of potion on a chain around my neck, tucked under my black sweater. I touched it now and then to feel the cool glass of the bottle. It was a solid reminder of what I had to do. I had to drink it. I had to forget.

Had to.

I squeezed it tightly and wished there was another choice, but I didn't want to be queen and I didn't want to die. There were no other choices.

"Thinking about tonight?" Melinda asked me at lunch.

I chewed on a french fry. I'd forgotten to pack a sandwich so fries and ketchup was my comfort food of the day.

I also had a Diet Coke to balance out the nutritional value, so no real harm was done.

"Tonight?" I repeated absently.

"Yeah, you know . . . the formal? Nikki, you are on another planet right now."

Actually more like another dimension, I thought. *A demon one.*

"Sorry, I'm a little distracted today." *To say the least.*

"Well, that's obvious." She sipped from her bottle of water and picked at her salad. "So I guess your stalker is long gone, huh?"

"My what?"

"Chris told me that he scared off your secret admirer yesterday. I guess it wasn't a practical joke after all. Too creepy. I wish you'd called me and told me about it."

I scanned the cafeteria. There was no sign of Michael lurking around. I hadn't seen him since last night.

Good night, not good-bye.

I cleared my throat. "Chris managed to get rid of him. I haven't seen the guy since," I lied. "I guess Chris can be sort of scary when he wants to be."

"Only because he cares about you." She squeezed my hand across the table. "You two make such a great couple. Am I, like, a total cupid or what?"

"You need a matchmaking license for how good you are." I smiled. "Any girl would be lucky to go out with Chris."

She tucked a long piece of light blonde hair behind her ear. "After everybody sees how great you look with Chris at the dance tonight, I'm sure you'll have lots of guys who want to stalk you. So you'd better get used to it."

I looked at her. "Gee, that's a comforting thought."

"Are you sure you're okay?"

"Never better."

Her smile faded around the edges. "Would you tell me if something's wrong? I mean, we are friends, right?"

I nodded. "Of course. Nothing's wrong."

"If you say so." She studied me for a moment and looked a bit disappointed that I wasn't telling her every single tidbit that took up space in my brain. "Listen, I'm ditching the rest of my classes to go to the salon. I have to look perfect tonight if I want to win the title of Queen. If you want your hair and makeup done, why don't you come with me?"

Another quick scan of the edges of the room confirmed that my stalker . . . or rather, Michael, was definitely nowhere to be seen.

"Thanks, but there's something I need to take care of," I said. "I need to go home."

"I guess I'll ask Larissa . . ." She glanced down the table at the bubbly brunette who would chew off her own arm to be Melinda's best friend. "You're not going to bail on the dance completely, are you? Because it's important that you're there. You have to be with me when I'm crowned Winter Queen."

I laughed at that. "Somebody's confident."

She smiled again and shrugged. "When you've got it, you've got it."

I sighed. "I still have no idea why you want to be my friend. I keep waiting for you to change your mind."

"That's strange, because I feel the same way about you."

"Obviously we're both pretty messed up."

"Tell me something I don't know."

I had no doubt in my mind that Melinda would take home her coveted prize tonight. She'd be Winter Queen. It was practically preordained. Like she'd been born into popularity, and it simply came naturally for her to dole it out at will to other people.

Like it was fate.

I'd been thinking about fate a lot since last night.

I touched the outline of the potion bottle under my shirt again.

I wished I could talk to my father. We hadn't had nearly enough time together. His demon form had scared me, badly, but I'd recovered. I wanted to see him again and get the chance to say a real good-bye. Michael would take me back there, wouldn't he? One last time before I drank the potion.

I craned my neck again. Where was Michael? I'd half-expected him to be waiting outside my house that morning, but he hadn't been there. I'd walked to school alone.

When the lunch period was over I stood up from the table, throwing my half-eaten fries into the garbage on my way out. I'd made my decision. I wasn't going to drink the potion until I'd had a chance to see my father again. But I knew it had to be soon. I knew there wasn't much time left.

My cell phone vibrated and I fished it out of my pocket. It was a text message.

hey gorgeous I hope ur ready for the best nite of ur life—prince charming

Chris. I rolled my eyes at his cute but cheesy message. My Prince Charming. He still was, I guessed. But his mega confidence wasn't nearly as appealing as it had been before.

I felt a bit guilty about leading him on when I had no intention of dating him anymore.

After all, he wasn't Michael.

I had to leave. I didn't want to be at school anymore, so I decided to skip my afternoon classes. I shifted my backpack to my other shoulder and left the school grounds, keeping one hand over the outline of my potion bottle while I walked.

"Michael?" I said out loud. "Where are you?"

A jogger headed in the opposite direction gave me a funny look.

Talking to myself. That must have looked really sane.

I crossed my arms and concentrated really hard.

Michael? I thought, trying to be all telepathic. *Are you there? Hello?*

There was no reply. Nothing.

My frustration gave way to a thread of worry. Where was he? Did he think I'd already taken the potion? Wasn't he coming back like he said he would?

Michael, if you're out there, please think something. Tell me you're okay.

I kept walking, but a little faster now. He'd said that the telepathy only worked when we were close to each other, hadn't he? I'd forgotten. It was one small piece of information in the sea of knowledge about the Shadowlands I was wading through. I was so confused.

Maybe he'd been punished for not telling me he was a servant. Maybe he wasn't allowed to contact me ever again.

I jogged down the hill leading into Hungry Hollow and over the little snow-covered bridge. The river was icy but it gurgled along underneath. Michael had been there twice waiting for me, watching over me. But he wasn't there today. That park had been the location of a lot of drama for me lately and I suddenly felt very alone and vulnerable.

Normally I would have thought I was just being all paranoid. Unfortunately, that wasn't the case.

The huge guy stepped out from behind the oak tree and blocked my path. It was the same one from yesterday—the one with the knife. The knife he still had.

"Princess," he greeted me.

Panic welled in my chest and I hoped that Michael would come marching down the path behind him, but there was nothing. Only the two of us stood in the middle of the empty park.

"Leave me alone," I told him and was surprised by how commanding I sounded.

"Can't do that, Princess. I have a job to do." His knife glinted. "As a Darkling, you have to die."

I'd been told I had to do a lot of things I didn't want to do lately—dying was right at the top of the list.

My throat tightened and I held up a hand. "But . . . I'm *not* a Darkling anymore. My father . . . the king . . . he gave me a potion and I drank it. I'm completely human now."

He studied me for a moment and then sniffed the air. "If that was the case, I would sense it. I don't smell only human. You're a liar."

I took a shaky step back from him. "Who are you?"

"It doesn't matter who I am. The only thing that matters is what I have to do."

"Where's Michael?" I demanded. My heart slammed against my ribcage and every muscle in my body was tense. "What have you done to him? Have you hurt him?"

"Who's Michael?"

"He was with me yesterday when you tried to attack me."

He narrowed his eyes. "The Shadow."

"Where is he?"

"I killed him."

I gasped. "No!"

His expression twisted into a cruel grin. "Just kidding, Princess. Why would I bother to kill a Shadow? But it's very interesting. A princess concerned for the fate of her servant. I'm sure the king wouldn't be too happy about that."

I felt like I was going to throw up. The thought that Michael could have been dead . . .

He eyed me then, his gaze moving down the length of me and changing from dangerous to leering. "You are very beautiful, Princess. I can see why your Shadow has developed a bond with you. It's unfortunate that I must destroy you now. I think we could have gotten along very nicely."

He closed the distance between us so fast that I didn't have a chance to move. He pressed the sharp knife against my throat.

Anger, panic, and fear surged simultaneously through me and my headache raged forward again so badly that my knees buckled.

"Don't do this," I managed as I grabbed his forearm, but he was like a tank. I knew I couldn't fight him off for very long. He was too strong.

But I *couldn't* just give up. I couldn't just let him kill me. I'd fight as much as I could for as long as I could. Past the fear, past the anger, past the panic. I concentrated all of my energy on doing whatever it took to get out of this alive.

My fear began to wash away from me like a sheet of water. I knew I should be scared. I should be begging for my life, but fear was suddenly the last thing on my mind.

I thought of my father, I thought of Michael. This couldn't be the end. I needed to see them again. One last time. The thought melded with the anger I felt and grew stronger and stronger.

I felt something very strange then. It was like somebody had lit a hundred sparklers inside of me. Little bursts of energy shot around in my stomach, only it didn't hurt. Actually, it felt pretty good. The sparks moved along my limbs, down my arms, and into my fingertips.

"I promise to make this quick, Princess," the brute said, so close to me now that along with feeling the painful sting of the knife at my throat, I could smell that he'd chosen not to use any form of deodorant that day.

I raised my eyes to his.

He growled. "No, Princess. You shouldn't do this."

"Shouldn't do what?"

"Your Darkling . . ." He began to loosen his grip on me.

"Darkling?" As I said it I sensed something shifting in my mouth. My teeth were changing. When I looked down at my hands, they remained my regular hands, but my fingernails grew to be long and black and pointed. I felt a rip, but it didn't hurt, and from the corners of my eyes I could see the black wings spread out from my back. Strength unlike anything I'd ever felt before welled inside of me, as if I were a kettle filled with boiling water about to start whistling loud enough for everyone in Erin Heights to hear.

I took a deep breath and realized that it didn't seem cold outside anymore. The temperature didn't bother me. I wasn't shivering from fear. As my attacker backed away from me, I stood straight and tall and energy hummed beneath the surface of my skin.

When I raised my hand I watched with amazement as a ball of energy formed and hovered an inch above my outstretched palm. The colors—red, orange, yellow—swirled and surged together faster and faster, the ball getting denser and denser the longer I concentrated on it.

Too cool.

The brute's eyes were wide as he watched me. Was that fear I saw in his expression? But then his eyes shifted to red—he was a demon, too, but still in human form—and he roared, clutching the knife tighter in his grip, and ran toward me. Without thinking, I threw the ball of energy at him. It hit him squarely in the chest. He flew backward and landed hard on the ground.

That's all it took. He was out cold.

I approached him in my demon form. I didn't feel completely in control of myself any longer—it was like something else had taken over. Something much more powerful, and something angry that anyone would try to attack me in the middle of a park. There was a car to my right at the edge of the parking lot and I walked past it so I could see my reflection in its windows. I tilted my head to the side and looked with shock at the demon-girl reflected back.

I looked different from my father. He'd been completely demon when he changed, but I was only half—a Darkling. My hair had changed from honey blonde to become red and long and flowing. It looked as if it was on fire, but it wasn't, which was a very good thing. My eyes were red and catlike, with no whites showing at all. My teeth weren't all sharp, only my canines—as though I wore fake vampire fangs.

Small, spiral horns emerged from just above my temples, red like my hair and shiny like metal. My talons were black and as sharp as X-acto blades. My wings stretched out behind me to their full width—about four feet on either side of me, black and leathery and perfect.

I still wore the clothes I'd left school in, as well as my winter coat, but it now had a huge gash in the back to make way for my wings. Underneath my clothes I could sense that lean muscle corded my arms and legs as if I were some kind of fitness model on ESPN. My hand glowed bright red from where I'd thrown the energy ball.

My eyes also glowed red like demonic lightbulbs.

Holy crap.

Being a Darkling made me feel different than I did in human form. I felt . . . bigger, better, stronger. And extremely dangerous to anyone who messed with me.

I reached down and felt at the unconscious brute's exposed neck. There was a pulse. Demons had pulses. This was very good to know.

He was still alive. Even though he wanted to kill me, that was also good to know.

Suddenly the power that had filled me left in a mind-numbingly painful *whoosh*. I braced myself against the tree as agony swept through me. My teeth returned to normal and my hands, too. The wings retracted and disappeared completely.

I felt utterly exhausted. In fact, I felt like collapsing to the ground, curling up into a ball, and falling unconscious for the next five years.

Elizabeth had told me not to harness my powers or I might die.

I'd just harnessed. Big-time. And the pain from it racked my body.

I doubled over and fell to my knees on the ground. It took me a minute before I could stand up again, stunned and amazed and scared beyond belief by what had just happened. I felt seriously ill. I needed to rest.

I'd just managed to save myself. But at what cost?

12

I was utterly convinced I was dying by the time I staggered home.

"Nikki," Mom called out as I made my way past her writing room. "Is that you?"

"Yeah, it's me," I replied weakly.

What could I tell her? I needed to get her to take me to the hospital. I didn't have much time. Elizabeth was right. I'd used my powers and now I was dying.

But instead of saying anything at all, I went directly to my room and closed the door. I knew what had to be done. I looked in the mirror on my vanity and saw a scared girl looking back at me. I didn't want to die.

Michael, I thought desperately. *Where are you?*

When there was no response I sat down on the edge of my bed and pulled the necklace out from under my shirt. I uncorked the vial of potion and held it up to my lips.

Drink it, I told myself. *Just drink it and get it over with.*

Get rid of the demon in me. Get rid of any trace of Darkling. Then what had happened wouldn't matter. I could get back to my normal life where the dance was the biggest thing I had to worry about. I could be normal. I didn't have to die.

Drinking the potion would solve all of my problems.

Do it. Do it now.

There was a knock at my door then and I pulled the bottle away from my mouth and jammed the stopper back into it.

"Nikki?" my mom said. "Is everything okay in there?"

"Fine," I managed.

"Can I come in?"

I tucked the bottle of potion under my tank top and pushed the tears off my cheeks. "Sure."

The door eased open and she looked in at me with concern.

I heard a male voice behind her. "What's going on?" It was Robert.

She glanced over her shoulder. "Nothing. Give us a minute, please."

He shuffled past the door and glared in at me. "Strong little thing, aren't you?" he said unpleasantly. His arm was in a cast now—the arm I broke like it was a pencil when he hit my mother.

"You have no idea." My eyes narrowed and I felt my headache return.

No, I thought. *I have to stay calm.* I couldn't risk my Darkling coming out again.

Robert didn't give any indication that he thought our altercation was anything more for me than a . . . well, a lucky *break*. I guess he hadn't noticed that my eyes had turned red. That was a relief.

When he'd left and I heard the door at the other end of the hallway click shut, I looked at my mom. "I thought he was staying with a friend?"

"He came back."

"I swear, Mom, if he hurts you again—"

She raised her hand. "I know, Nikki. Don't worry. It's not going to happen again. I won't let it." She leaned against the wall. "I was worried that you were sick coming home early today. But you actually look wonderful."

"I do?"

She nodded.

I sure didn't feel wonderful. I frowned at the thought. Then again, I didn't feel *that* bad anymore. The pain was starting to fade away to nearly nothing at all.

"I brought you something." She entered my bedroom fully so I could see she held a paperback novel in her hand. "It's the new one. I just got my copies today. I think you'll like it."

I took it from her and checked out the darkly good-looking cover model staring at me. I ran my finger along the embossing on her name. "What's it about?"

"It's about a handsome vampire and a beautiful woman who was his wife hundreds of years ago. She's been reincarnated so she doesn't quite remember him, but in her soul she knows that she's always loved him."

I thought about my father and how he'd loved my

mother before being parted from her. How he was trapped inside the castle and now was going to die all alone.

"Does it have a happy ending?" I asked.

"Of course." She smiled. "I wouldn't have it any other way."

I put the book on my bedside table. "I really want you to have a happy ending, too, Mom."

She sat next to me on the bed and put her arm around me. "Happy endings only happen for characters in books. The rest of us have to deal with reality."

I'd begun to slowly relax now that my brush with death had officially passed. I'd been so scared that I'd almost drunk the potion. If my mom hadn't stopped me . . . I'd already be forgetting everything.

Then I wondered if that would have been so bad. Mom was right. Happy endings weren't that realistic—not in my case, anyway.

"Maybe you just haven't found your handsome vampire yet," I said.

She scrunched her nose. "Not sure I'd go for a vampire. I hate the sight of blood."

"But since you write about them, you must think that . . . *monsters* . . . are kind of sexy, right?"

It was a baited question, I'll admit it. If my father could have had his chance to tell her his secrets, what would she have done? Would she have run screaming from the room at his demon form? Or would she have loved him anyway?

I didn't know. I guessed I'd never know.

She shook her head. "It's just a book, honey. It's not like monsters actually exist."

"Right." I cleared my throat. "Forget about it."

After another minute she left my room to get her dress for me to borrow. I wanted to tell her that I wasn't going to the dance. Winter Formal was the last thing I wanted to think about, but again I didn't say anything.

I was tired. So tired.

I put my head down on my pillow and even though my brain was going a million miles a minute, I fell asleep right away.

When I woke up it was because my mom was yelling up the stairs for me. "Nikki! Melinda's on the phone for you!"

I sat up and rubbed my eyes and then looked at the clock. It was nearly six thirty. I'd just slept for four hours.

Not good.

I grabbed for the receiver and held it to my ear. "Melinda?" My voice came out all croaky.

"Please tell me you're almost ready," she said simply.

I swallowed hard. "Not exactly."

"You're bailing on the dance, aren't you?" She sounded mad.

"I . . . I don't really think I'm feeling so great—I'm coming down with something. It's probably better if I just stay home."

There was a long pause. "Is it because you're not into Chris anymore?"

I sighed. "That has a little to do with it, but it's not the only reason."

Another long pause. "I don't understand what's going on with you."

"Look, Melinda, you'll have a good time tonight. Everybody will be there. You won't even notice that I'm missing."

She didn't say anything for a moment, but I could hear a muffled sound.

"Why are you crying?"

"I'm not crying. That's ridiculous." She sniffed.

"What's wrong?"

"It's okay, Nikki," she said. "I get it. You don't want to be my friend. It's fine. It would help if you just came right out and said it."

"Melinda, that isn't what I'm saying."

"It's just . . . I don't know. This town . . . everybody is so fake."

"That's not true."

"It is. Larissa is super friendly, but I know she's just using me, too, like today with getting her hair and makeup done. She wants to be friends with the popularity, not with me. She even passed my screening process, but she's just like the rest of them."

I couldn't exactly argue that one. "She's not *that* bad."

"You have to come to the dance. I'm stressed out about Winter Queen. I have to win and you have to be there with me."

I racked my brain for another excuse, but I couldn't exactly tell her the truth, could I?

Definitely not.

"Please, Nikki." There was an odd tone of desperation and loneliness to her words. Who would ever believe that the most popular girl in Erin Heights had issues with insecurity? "You don't have to stay all night. Just an hour or two."

"You do know how needy you sound, right?"

She laughed a little at that. "It's pathetic, I know. Don't make me beg. It won't be pretty."

I let out a long sigh and looked at the dress hanging from my closet door—the one that my mom must have delivered during my four-hour power nap. "Okay. Fine. I'll go."

"Then get dressed! And hurry up, we've got to be there in an hour."

Great. Just great.

I hung up the phone and tried to relax. The last thing I needed right now was to turn Darkling again. After a few minutes, I forced myself to put everything out of my mind. I then ran to take the shortest shower of my life. After blow-drying my hair, I quickly attempted an updo that surprisingly worked out better than expected.

When I finished with my makeup, I grabbed the Austrian crystal earrings Mom had gotten me as a birthday present and put them on. Last but not least, I slipped the gorgeous, spaghetti-strapped, backless lavender silk dress over my head and felt the luxurious material skim along my skin as it fell into place.

I also borrowed my mom's heels—silver strappy designer

heels not terribly appropriate for December weather, but they looked fantastic with the dress. I finished right at the stroke of seven o'clock, just as the doorbell rang.

The limo was here to pick me up.

A last peek in my vanity mirror showed a wild-eyed blonde girl wearing a beautiful dress. I took a quick, shallow breath that sounded shaky at best.

I would go because Melinda, my crazy, overdramatic, popular-on-the-outside best friend wanted me to.

I would try to be normal.

I would try not to think about my father. I would try to forget about Michael.

But I knew there was only one way for me to truly forget. One way for me to truly be normal.

I had to drink the potion.

I picked up the small bottle from the table next to my discarded makeup and stared at it for a moment.

Another quick glance at the mirror reflected a girl holding a small innocuous-looking bottle, her hazel, black-rimmed eyes shiny with tears, as she contemplated forever wiping away the memory that she was a demon princess.

Drink it.

My gaze narrowed at my reflection.

I'll drink it later.

I slipped the bottle into my purse and headed out to the limo.

13

Chris wore a tuxedo that looked tailor-made for him. Since his family was wealthy, it probably had been. Honestly, the guy was absolutely gorgeous. Perfect hair, perfect face, perfect body. He smiled when he saw me—a perfect smile.

"Wow," he said. "Nikki, you look amazing."

"Thanks." I gave him a weak smile. It wasn't his fault that, despite his perfection, I wasn't head-over-heels in love with him. But I wouldn't tell him tonight. In the end, it wouldn't matter anyway. He'd have no problem finding somebody else who would be beyond thrilled to date him.

But who knew? When I took the potion I might feel about Chris like I had before.

After I forgot about Michael.

I swallowed past the big lump in my throat as I remembered kissing him last night.

Good night, not good-bye.

I wished I could have seen him again. So much.

Chris led me out to the limo where Melinda was waiting with her date, a college freshman named Stephen whose full attention was currently on his BlackBerry. Melinda, as expected, looked absolutely stunning in a full-length red dress fit for a potential Winter Queen.

"When can we leave this thing?" Stephen asked, tucking the BlackBerry into his inner jacket pocket. He wasn't as good-looking as Chris. In fact, I thought he resembled a thin-faced rat. I had absolutely no idea what Melinda saw in him. "There's a big party at my frat house tonight."

Melinda sighed. "Does no one except me want to go to the dance tonight?"

"I do," Chris said quickly.

Stephen snorted. "Maybe Nikki and I should hang out and leave you two to your lame dance."

I grimaced. *Well, that was unlikely.*

I stared out the limo window for the rest of the short ride and tried to remain calm, cool, and collected. The limo came to a stop in front of the high school and it was a blur getting out. Chris took my hand in his and pulled me along behind him through the crowd of people milling around outside. They parted like the Red Sea to let us through. It was seriously surreal.

I was surrounded by hundreds of happy, excited people and I'd never felt so alone.

The rest of the Royal Party bounded toward us with their dates—all of them Chris's friends—trailing behind as if attached by invisible wires.

"Melinda, you look gorgeous!"

"Your hair . . . it's fabulous!"

"You are *so* going to be Winter Queen!"

Melinda turned to me and rolled her eyes so only I could see it. That made me smile a little.

"Let's get inside," Chris said. "It's freezing out here."

Funny. I hadn't even noticed.

I wasn't wearing a jacket. Mom had wanted me to, but it was only a short walk from the limo to the inside of the school, and besides, no one else was wearing a coat. Call me stubborn.

I wondered if that was another trait I shared with my father.

Inside, the decorating committee had done a fantastic job of turning the gym into a magical place. They'd spared no expense. At my last school in San Diego, before Mom married Robert and I had to transfer to Erin Heights, dances hadn't been such a big deal, but here they were the ultimate event. And they treated it that way, both the students and the teachers. When this one was over they'd immediately start planning the next one, trying to outdo what they'd done tonight.

That would be difficult. All my troubles were momentarily swept away as the flickering lights that sprinkled across the dance floor washed over me. The walls had been covered in dark blue fabric. The ceiling hung with streamers that sparkled as the light caught them. There were tables all around the edges of the dance floor, draped in shimmering cloth. Even the chairs were covered with ribbons and drapery to hide their utilitarian outsides. The deejay had set up to the left side of the stage where the Winter King and Queen would be crowned. To the far right was a long buffet table holding hors d'oeuvres, pastries, bottles of water, and a big bowl of red fruit punch.

Everyone in attendance looked stunning. It was like they'd spent hours getting ready, which was—according to how empty the school had been that afternoon before I left—probably an accurate assessment.

Each table had an ornate centerpiece of flowers, paper snowflakes, and balloons. It sounded tacky, but somehow it managed to look elegant. The balloons were white and silver and bore the imprint "Winter Magic."

It did feel magical.

But I still didn't want to be there.

I absently touched my dragon's tear bracelet, twisting it around and around.

I'd stay for an hour and then I'd make my excuses to leave. When I got home I'd drink the potion. I'd decided once and for all.

Melinda came to my side and reached down to squeeze my hand. She wore a big smile. "I won't forget this, Nikki. Thank you for coming. I'm so glad you moved to Erin Heights."

I laughed a little. "You're just saying that because I saved you from choking."

She shook her head. "See . . . that was fate. If that hadn't happened I might never have gotten to know you." She frowned. "Well, also I'd probably be dead. But I just feel like I can trust you. That you'd tell me anything."

"Well . . ."

She raised her eyebrows. "What?"

"If I am being perfectly honest . . ."

"Yes?"

"I think your new boyfriend is a jerk."

She sighed. "I think you might be right about that."

"No, actually, I know I am. He's hitting on Larissa right now."

She turned her head to see Stephen with his hand braced against the wall behind the brunette in question—the same one who'd spent all afternoon with Melinda getting gorgeous. Larissa looked up at Stephen as if he was a movie star. He tucked a strand of dark hair behind her ear. She giggled.

"Well, that's unfortunate," Melinda said out loud.

"Sorry."

She gave a small shrug. "Don't be. Guys are a dime a dozen, but real friends are way harder to find."

"You sound like a Hallmark card."

"My parents want me to be a doctor, but that's what I'm really going to do after high school. Be a writer for greeting cards." Her smile faded and she sighed shakily. "Things are difficult for me right now, Nikki. Nobody knows. Maybe that's why I want tonight to be as perfect as possible. It might be my last chance to be completely normal."

I looked at her intently. I guess we really *did* have more in common than I thought. After all, I'm sure I was the least normal person in the entire room. Possibly the entire world. "What's wrong?"

She shook her head. "I can't talk about it."

"I'm having some issues, too." *To say the least.*

"With Chris?"

I glanced over in his direction. Chris was laughing with one of his friends. "No, it doesn't have anything to do with him."

She raised an eyebrow. "Well, if you tell me yours, I *might* tell you mine."

Melinda looked so open, so curious, and hopeful that I'd share my big secret, that right then and there I decided to tell her. I'd only known her for a couple of months, but if anyone might be able to help me deal with my problems, it just might be her. I trusted her. It would be a huge weight off my shoulders if I could share it with somebody.

"Well . . . ," I said, looking around our immediate surroundings to make sure no one was listening in. "I just found out I'm a half-demon princess."

Then I clamped my mouth shut. It sounded just as crazy as it did in my head, and the look on her face—sort of a stunned confusion as if that was the last thing she ever expected me to say—was enough to make me wish I hadn't said anything at all. Was it too late to take it back?

I cleared my throat nervously and tried to grin at her. "I'm kidding, of course."

Thankfully, that brought a smile to her face again. "Well, it's good that you're kidding because I just found out that I'm a demon slayer, so I'd probably have to kill you." She went quiet for a moment. "I'm kidding, too, of course."

"Funny." I forced a laugh.

Although, I didn't think it was *that* funny. In fact, the idea that she was even remotely serious made me feel sick to my stomach.

I tried to put it out of my mind. After all, Melinda sure didn't look like somebody who might spend her spare time slaying demons.

Then again, at the moment I didn't look all that royally demonic.

A half hour later, Melinda was crowned Winter Queen. No big surprise there. The surprise was that Chris was crowned Winter King—despite my previous mega crush on him, I didn't even know he was up for the title. After the announcement, he wore the crown, tipped with little plastic snowflakes, proudly.

"I'm king," he kept saying.

"Congrats."

"We can leave now, if you want. We'll get the limo to swing by your house. I get the feeling that you're not having much fun."

I was a terrible actress. Despite wanting to forget about Michael and about everything else, I was failing horribly. My problems hadn't left my mind for a moment.

The fact that Chris had noticed and didn't want to force me to stay any longer earned him significant bonus points. I'd go home and try to contact Michael one last time. But after that . . . drinking the potion was my only option.

Fate. It was all about fate.

"Thanks," I said to Chris.

"Let's go."

I said good-bye to Melinda and some of the other members of the Royal Party. Then Chris took my hand and led me across the dance floor and out of the gym completely. After a moment we were back outside in the cold air. Was it this cold when we'd arrived? It had to be below zero out there. The sky was dark and clear and I could see the constellations overhead that Mom always pointed out to me when I was a little girl, although now I knew that she'd been making most of them up.

The limo was parked to the side of the parking lot near a long fence, but the driver was nowhere to be seen.

"We'll wait inside until he gets back," Chris suggested.

I wrapped my bare arms around myself and rubbed them to try to warm up. Chris opened the back door and disappeared inside. After a moment, I joined him. Once I was in, he reached over and pulled the door closed behind me.

Yes, it was much warmer in there. But dark. I could see out, but I knew the tinted glass meant that no one could see in. It was silent and peaceful and I could finally think clearly away from the loud, throbbing music in the gym.

Chris patted the seat next to him. "Come and sit next to me. You look frozen."

I sighed, but moved over to him. Getting closer to him helped warm me immediately.

"Lame dance, right?" he said.

I shook my head. "The dance was great. I . . . I'm just not feeling up to it tonight."

"Why not?"

I pressed back in the seat. "I've been dealing with some problems this week."

"Like what?"

"Like"—I hesitated—"like, I found out that my father is dying."

"Oh, my God, Nikki. That's terrible."

And then I started to cry. Just like that. One moment I wasn't and then the next moment I was. Great big fat tears slipped down my cheeks and I covered my face with my hands.

Chris touched my shoulder and then pulled me toward him in a comforting hug against his chest. I leaned into him and hugged him back, letting it out while he held me.

"Nikki," he murmured against my hair. "It's okay."

I shook my head. No, it wasn't okay. My father was going to die. I'd just met him and now he was going to be gone and I couldn't believe how much I was going to miss him.

Chris drew me even closer to him. I could feel the thud of his heart through his tuxedo shirt.

"It's okay," he continued to say for a few minutes, holding me. And then, "Oh, Nikki, you are so damn hot in that dress."

I frowned and pulled away a little, my vision blurry from the tears. "What did you say?"

"You like me, right?"

"Of course I like you—"

"Good." He kissed me.

I braced my hands against his chest and managed to pull back a little. "Chris, I think I need to go."

"I thought you said you liked me."

"I do, but this isn't right. I want to leave. I can call my mom for a ride."

"You liked it when I kissed you yesterday."

I sighed. He was right. I did like it. But a lot of things had changed since yesterday.

"I'm sorry," I said. "This has nothing to do with you. You're a great guy, really, but . . . I don't know. I just need to be alone right now."

"You're alone," he said. "With me."

"That's not exactly what I meant."

His eyes were heavy lidded, his lips moist. I could now smell alcohol on his breath even though I hadn't seen him drink anything. He wasn't looking in my eyes, his gaze was sliding down to my chest.

"Come on," he said. "You, me, a limo. This is the chance we've been waiting for to get to know each other a little better."

I couldn't even talk anymore because his noodle lips were on me again. This time, if possible, even harder than before. He pushed his tongue into my mouth and I felt like gagging. In fact, I think I did. I pushed at his chest, but the guy was strong.

His hands were everywhere then, and he pushed me down on the seats so he was on top of me, his body weight easily holding me down. I started to panic. I knew what he wanted to do. Something I hadn't done before and was frankly in no hurry to start. Not with him. And not like this.

"No! Chris, get off of me!"

He frowned, seeming not to understand why I was getting mad. "I know you want me," he growled. "Melinda told me you have a crush on me. That's why I asked you out. Don't try to play hard to get now. You like me and I like you. What's the problem?"

He mashed his mouth against mine again.

Panic gave way to fear.

"Stop it!" I beat at his chest. He grabbed my wrists and held them down on either side of my head.

Had no one ever said no to Chris before? Was he so used to getting what he wanted, because he was popular and handsome and rich, that now he didn't get it when I said no?

I'd thought he was so nice.

But there was nothing nice about him at the moment. It was a surprise, a shock, and a total disappointment.

Those are all the things I would have been feeling if I hadn't been so scared.

"I thought you wanted to be popular." There was a gleam in his eyes then. A sick satisfaction at having me sprawled out under him, helpless, in the back of a limo, no less. "I want you to be my girlfriend. It's a total honor, in case you didn't know. Now don't screw it up. This is going to happen. You can have a good time or a bad time, but it's going to happen."

He kissed me again, hard.

My fear suddenly shifted to anger—a hot line of fury that welled up inside of me just waiting to erupt. My head screamed out in pain.

I bit his bottom lip. He snarled and backed up, raising his hand as if to slap me.

But he stopped.

His expression changed from lust and amusement to something else.

Fear.

I could tell because of the bright red light shining on his face.

The red light from my glowing demon eyes.

14

As odd as it sounds, I could smell Chris's fear as it radiated off him in waves. It smelled sweet, like melting ice cream.

"A good time or a bad time, huh?" I sat up and out of the corners of my eyes I could see the big, black wings stretch out behind me. I liked how my voice sounded. Deeper, drier, and extremely scary. "I think I choose a bad time—for *you*."

The blast of light from my energy ball exploded a limo door right off its hinges and Chris was launched out after it, landing hard on his back on the pavement of the parking lot.

I got out of the limo easily as strength and power filled every inch of my body. It was dark, but I could see perfectly. The outlines of objects were sharp and defined. I looked down at the black talons protruding from the tips of my fingers. I ran my tongue along my fangs. I didn't need a mirror to tell me that I looked positively demonic. A Darkling. A furious, black-winged, spiral-horned, red-haired monster in a borrowed backless Versace dress and silver strappy heels.

The cold didn't bother me at all anymore.

The glow from my eyes tracked over to where Chris lay on the ground. He shook his head as he looked at me with wide eyes, then crawled backward, crablike, to get away.

"N-no, p-please," he stuttered. "P-please don't hurt me."

"Exactly what part of 'no' didn't you understand?" I asked, seething with anger.

He whimpered.

I was disappointed in him. So horribly disappointed. He was supposed to be perfect—good-looking, popular, a nice guy all around. He wasn't the right person for me, I already knew that. But this? I hadn't expected this from the guy I'd been crushing on for two months.

"Wh-what are you?" he stammered.

I cocked my head to the side. "What do you mean?"

"You're a *monster*."

I cringed. The last thing I needed was him to tell anybody about this. "You're drunk, Chris. Maybe somebody slipped you something stronger than alcohol. You're obviously imagining things."

"I . . . I am?"

"That's right." I glared down at him. "And when you wake up tomorrow you'll realize this was all just a drunken hallucination." I hesitated. "But remember this . . . never come near me again. I don't think that'll be much of a problem for you, will it? But listen to me very closely. I know you're used to getting what you want, but if I ever hear that you've tried to hurt anyone else?" I bared my fangs and watched the fear flood his expression. "You will be very, very sorry. Do you understand me?"

He whimpered again pathetically.

"Do you understand?" I asked again, raising my scary voice up a notch.

"Y-y-yes. I understand. I do. I . . . I promise."

I hissed out a breath. "Then I think this date is officially over."

He nodded in complete and total agreement.

"You need to go home now." It wasn't a magical demonic suggestion that he couldn't resist. It was simply a suggestion.

One he took.

He was gone.

Whether Chris had been drunk or not, I had a sick feeling that what he had just seen wouldn't be forgotten quite as easily as I hoped it would be.

Once he had disappeared into the distance, running along the street in the direction of his home, I took in a very shaky breath and realized I was trembling violently.

I might have sounded all cool with him, but inside a storm was raging. I was furious and beyond upset. The anger at what he'd attempted to do to me swirled around my stomach making me nauseous. I felt the overwhelming need to cry or destroy something.

Possibly both.

Relax, Nikki, I told myself. *You have to relax.*

If I didn't calm myself down, I knew something horrible was going to happen.

Energy sparked off the ends of my black talons. My heart pounded so hard in my chest I could feel it and hear it in my ears, a loud, thunderous sound. I couldn't seem to relax. The rage I was feeling was spiraling inside of me. I felt out of control.

Then a hand curled over my bare shoulder. I flexed my leathery wings and whipped my head to the side, ready to hurt whoever stood there.

It was Michael.

His eyes widened as he took a moment to look at me. Then he blinked.

"Come on," he said. "It's not safe here."

He grabbed my wrist and pulled me along with him around the corner to a vacant side of the school. I didn't resist but my shaking was getting even worse.

"I can't control this," I gasped.

"Sure you can." He stopped walking and turned to face me. "Just breathe."

I nodded and a lock of bright, flame-red hair fell onto my face. Michael stroked it back. I was surprised he'd want to touch me when I was like this.

"Demon form can be triggered from feeling high emotions like anger or fear." He frowned deeply. "I saw Chris leave here. He didn't . . . he didn't try to hurt you, did he?"

I sucked in a shaky breath. "He cornered me in the back of a limo and wouldn't take no for an answer, if you know what I mean."

"He *what*?" What felt like an actual wave of fury radiated off Michael and it made goose bumps crawl over my skin. "He tried to . . . to . . . ? I'm going to *kill him*. I will tear the head from his body!"

I shook my head. "No, I'm okay. After he's seen me

like this I'm sure he won't come anywhere near me ever again. I scared the crap out of him."

His expression was tense and angry, but he gently wiped a tear from my cheek with his thumb. "You're really okay?"

My breath was still coming in quick gasps. "Except . . . except for this demon thing. I couldn't control it. And now I can't change back. Of course I was able to scare Chris off. I scared him by how ugly I am."

He shook his head. "Princess, there's nothing ugly about you." He cupped my face in his hands. "But you have to try to relax."

I had to relax. I *had* to.

Pain radiated through my stomach. "I'm dying. Harnessing my Darkling powers is killing me."

"You're not dying." He hugged me to him a lot like how Chris had in the limo, but it was different now. Michael wasn't Chris. I hadn't known Michael for very long at all, but I knew he wouldn't hurt me. Holding on to him helped me to slowly calm down. It made me feel safe. It helped chase away the anger and fear.

"Shh, it's okay." He kissed my cheek and stroked my hair back from my face.

I closed my eyes and held on to him, and slowly I felt the Darkling inside of me recede. My wings began to disappear. My teeth desharpened. My nails returned to their short, pink-polished state. The pain grew worse but as I returned to normal and clung to Michael I realized it wasn't as bad as the last time I changed back to human form.

"Better?" he asked after a few minutes went by.

I nodded. He began to pull away from me but I held on tight.

He looked down into my eyes. "See? You're not dead."

"Not yet." I took a deep breath. The pain was completely gone now and it gave me a chance to think straight. I looked up at him. "Where were you all day? I thought you said you'd come to see me again."

"I know. I'm sorry, I couldn't come before now."

"Why not?"

His expression shadowed. "I just couldn't. I . . . I thought you would have drunk the potion by now."

"But you came anyway?"

"I wanted to make sure you were all right. You had mentioned the dance so I knew you'd be here at the school." He must have seen the hurt look that I couldn't hide and he swallowed hard. "I wanted to come earlier. I did. I'm really sorry I wasn't here for you."

"But you're here now. Thank you for helping me calm down."

"You're very welcome." He smiled a little and then turned more serious. "You should have drunk the potion by now, though. The king . . . he's getting worse." He exhaled. "Elizabeth thinks he has only hours left, not days."

My heart twisted. "I need to see him again."

He shook his head. "That's not a good idea."

"Why not?"

"Taking you back to the Shadowlands would only make it harder. For you, for your father. He's in no shape to see anyone—he's constantly in demon form now. And there's no time left. You . . . you have to drink the potion or you won't have any choice when the king dies. You'll automatically become queen. I know you don't want that."

"And I don't want to die."

"Die?" he asked. "What are you talking about?"

"Elizabeth told me that harnessing my Darkling powers will kill me. I've done it three times now and I guess I've gotten off lucky." I swallowed. "I can't let it happen again."

He looked confused. "She told you that?"

I nodded. "She researched Darklings when my father asked her to. She didn't want to tell him or it would worry him more."

His brow lowered. "What do you mean you've turned Darkling *three times?*"

I quickly told him about my confrontation with knife-guy again in the park. His expression grew darker with every word.

"I should have been there for you," he said. "I should have protected you."

"It's okay."

"No, it's not. You were in danger and I didn't help you. But Elizabeth . . ." He paused. "She cares very much what happens to you. And she's very adamant that you drink the potion—she says it's the only way. She allowed me to come back here to check if you had or not." He met my eyes and his expression was strained. "You have to drink it, Nikki."

My throat thickened. "Do you really want me to forget about you?"

"It's the only way."

"You keep saying that. But it doesn't answer my question."

He looked down at the ground. "Princess, I'm a servant. I'm not supposed to want things."

"You don't act like a servant."

"Then I'm very sorry," he said. "But I'm just supposed to do what I'm told without questioning it. It's the only way I've ever known."

Something about how he said it made me think very hard. Servants couldn't question orders given to them. They had to do what others told them because . . . because why? They weren't supposed to have minds of their own. Not allowed to make their own decisions, whether that decision was right or wrong.

Sounded like being a teenager. Everybody told me what to do. Where to move. What classes to take, what tests to study for. What books to read.

And now I was being told to drink a potion because there was no other way. Elizabeth's argument for me drinking it was a very good one, though. I didn't want to die. I didn't want to be queen.

No other choice.

"For what it's worth," Michael said after a moment of silence between us, "I don't want you to forget about me. And if things were at all different, I'd tell you not to drink the potion if you didn't really want to. But that would be selfish and stupid of me."

I shook my head. "It's not stupid. Or selfish."

He met my gaze again and held it. "When King Desmond first told me to come here to the human realm, to find his daughter and bring her back to see him, I was convinced you'd be a spoiled brat. I thought that as soon as you found out I was your servant you'd treat me like a nobody. That's the reason I didn't tell you what I was until you found out from your father. When we were in the alleyway after that guy attacked you, and you didn't leave me there—you waited, you stayed with me until I was better—I didn't feel like a nobody. I didn't want to lose that."

"You're *not* a nobody," I told him, swallowing past the huge lump in my throat.

"My parents died when I was young and your father has treated me well. I can't really complain too much. But it's not the same as . . . as how you treat me. You surprised me, Princess. So much. And when you kissed me last night . . ." He pressed his lips together.

I waited as my heart drummed loudly.

He blinked. "Everything changed."

I inhaled sharply. "What does that mean?"

"It means I don't want you to take the potion and forget about me. It means even though I know who I am and who you are I still want to kiss you again right now. So badly." His mouth was close to mine and he stroked my back-to-blonde hair off my face. "But I can't."

He pulled back and reached down the front of his shirt to pull his amulet out. Only then did I realize he'd had it tucked inside his shirt before.

"Why not?"

"Because your father wanted me to protect you, and that's what I'm going to do." He turned and looked away. "That's why you have to drink the potion. When you do that, you'll be safe."

It was silent then between us as I thought about everything Michael had just told me. Why did this have to be so hard?

"You said my father only has hours left," I said.

He nodded gravely.

"I want to see him."

"I already told you that's not a very good idea."

"I heard you. But I don't care. I want you to take me to him and Elizabeth again. Please."

"Princess. Please, drink the potion now. It's for your own protection."

"No."

His gaze snapped to mine. "No?"

I set my jaw. "That's right. I know everybody wants me to drink it, and I'm going to, eventually. But I want to see my father first, or else I'll refuse to drink it at all. I want to go back to the Shadowlands to see him one last time. Please help me do that."

"You'd put yourself at personal risk to make this happen?"

I crossed my arms. "Looks like."

"And if I still refuse?"

I slowly let out a shaky breath. "My father said that you were supposed to do as I asked. Isn't that true?"

He grimaced. I hated having to remind him of his servant status. I didn't think of him that way—not even slightly. But I needed him to take me back without arguing. Even though commanding him to do it made me feel sick inside.

"Of course it's true, Princess." He looked away. "If you order me to take you back, then there is nothing I can do but take you."

I forced myself not to cry. "Then I order you to take me back to the Shadowlands."

"Very well." He nodded slowly. "We should leave immediately."

"I need five minutes first. I have to go inside and say good-bye to my friends or they'll be worried about me."

He didn't look directly at me. "I'll wait here."

Heavy-hearted, I stopped at the limo first and retrieved my purse through the opening where the door had blown off. I'd placed the potion bottle inside it since I couldn't hide it under the low neckline of my dress. I went inside the school, and into the gym. I'd already said good-bye to Melinda earlier so that wasn't actually my main reason for going back.

Instead, I went to the bathroom and stared at my now-disheveled reflection in the mirror over the sinks. At least

I didn't see any remaining traces of Darkling. I'd fully turned Darkling twice—three times if you counted what happened to Robert—and I was still alive, still breathing. Maybe Elizabeth was wrong. Maybe I was different from the other Darklings she'd researched.

I tried to smooth my now-messy updo back into place. I splashed cold water on my face and touched up what little of my makeup was left as best as I could. I dug into my purse to get my lipstick and my fingers grazed the bottle of potion. I pulled it out and looked at it for a long moment, a million possibilities racing through my mind.

If I drank it everything would be normal again.

But what was normal anymore?

Michael didn't want me to drink it but he said I had to.

Sounded exactly how I felt about it, too.

Didn't want to, but *had to*.

I was so sick of being told what I had to do. It was usually the exact opposite of what I *wanted* to do.

I stared at my reflection for a couple more minutes, trying to will something deep inside of me to the surface. Courage, inner strength, serenity, something that would help me to do what I knew then, without a shadow of a doubt, I had to do.

After another minute, I left the bathroom and walked to the punch bowl to get a glass of the fruity beverage. Drinking it made me feel momentarily better. I hadn't realized how thirsty I was. I looked down into the bowl as the orange slices swam on top, and I tried to collect my thoughts. I wanted to get rid of the feeling of dread that swirled violently in my head—not unlike the dark storm clouds beginning to circle over the school, threatening snow.

A storm was brewing and I was headed right toward it.

But no one seemed to notice but me.

15

I seriously wished I'd taken a coat to the dance. Little did I know I'd be walking through Erin Heights in a spaghetti-strapped silk dress and bare legs in the middle of December. Luckily, it wasn't snowing yet, but I was still chilled to the bone.

Michael noticed I was shivering and immediately gave me his hooded sweatshirt to wear. Otherwise he was quiet.

"Thank you," I said, zipping it up over my dress. I still felt horrible that I had ordered him around. "Look . . . I'm sorry about this. Really."

"Forget it," he said quietly.

But I *didn't* want to forget. That was one of the reasons I was going back to the Shadowlands. I was sure there had to be a way for everything to work out without taking the potion.

I knew I'd made some potentially questionable decisions. I just hoped it would all work out for the best.

"Do me a favor, though?" he asked after another minute. "Don't tell Elizabeth you've turned Darkling. It will . . . it will worry her too much."

He was right about that. I wouldn't tell her. But she was the resident expert on Darklings. I had to talk to her and get more of an idea of what I was up against.

Besides, if she was willing to be queen and I didn't want the position, why couldn't it be left at that? A decision rather than an uncontrollable selection process that couldn't be changed?

I looked at Michael. I could tell that he was trying to sense where we could find another gateway. His amulet pulsed with dim light.

"My father told me that if Shadows still ruled the Shadowlands you'd be a prince," I said. "Is that true?" I wasn't sure where the question came from, but I had to ask.

He kept his eyes on the sidewalk ahead of him. "Yeah. But they don't and I'm not, so it doesn't really matter, does it?" His amulet flared with green light. He turned right once we entered the downtown area. "Here's where we want to go."

Behind the convenience store where Mom usually picked up milk and scratch-and-win lottery tickets, Michael took hold of a large Dumpster and pulled it away from the wall an inch or two. Behind it I could see a dull glow.

"That's a gateway?" I asked.

He nodded. "They're well hidden in the human realm and they shift regularly. We wouldn't want just anyone accidentally dropping into another dimension, would we?"

"No, that would be very bad."

Once he'd pulled the Dumpster completely away from the wall and I could see the outline of the gateway clearly, he turned to me with a concerned expression. "Look, I'm doing this for you against my will. I want you to know this. You shouldn't go back there. You should drink the potion and be safe here. But you want to go and so I'm taking you. Just . . . just be careful, okay?"

I'd expected him to still be mad at me for pulling rank and this strange concern was surprising. I swallowed hard. "Okay."

He fixed me with a grim look that softened the longer he gazed into my eyes. And then he turned around and disappeared through the glowing gateway. I didn't wait too long. I followed, experiencing the lurch and vertigo of my previous gateway trip. The next moment I stood on the threshold of the Shadowlands, with the faery realm next to me, warm and green and beautiful.

Well, here I am again, I thought, as the stunned realization sunk in that I was really back. The vertigo stayed a moment longer than last time and I wobbled in my high heels. Michael put his arm around my waist to steady me. After I regained my equilibrium, I took off his sweatshirt and handed it back to him. Our fingers brushed as he took it from me and then he slowly gazed at my lavender dress, which he could now see in daylight.

"You look so beautiful, Princess," he said.

A breath caught in my chest. I normally would have been thrilled with a compliment from him, but he said it so sadly and when he looked in my eyes, he seemed worried.

He was afraid. Of what, exactly? Of bringing me back

here unannounced and getting in trouble? Of my father dying and my being trapped here as a very unwilling queen? I was afraid of that, too. More than he knew.

Or was it something else entirely?

Before I could ask, he turned away from me. "Let's go."

My high heels dug into the soft ground as we walked, but once the ground turned to gray rock it was a bit better, although still precarious. The front doors of Castle Dread opened for us when we finally reached them and a chill went down my spine as I entered the now-familiar expansive front area with its glistening black floor and spiral staircase.

I felt a wave of fear then, but I knew there was no time for that. I wanted to see my father, I wanted to talk to my aunt. Now, before it was too late.

My feet were killing me. Heels were great for sitting in a limo and hanging out at a dance, but obviously not so good for interdimensional travel. I took a minute to take them off and leave them by the front door, preferring to walk around on the cool, smooth floors in bare feet than to continue with my self-inflicted torture.

"Where's Elizabeth?" I asked.

"She's probably in her quarters," Michael said as we began making our way up the stairs. At the top I reached for his hand and he glanced at me with surprise.

"You don't mind?" I asked.

"Of course not."

We walked past the large, cavernous room with the fireplace that I remembered very clearly from last night, and then down a hall, deeper into the castle. Instead of electric lights, there were candles and oil lamps on the walls. The flames flickered in the darkness to light the hallway.

Michael glanced at me. "You're sure you really want to be here?"

"Of course. Why?"

"Because you're practically squeezing my hand off my wrist."

I cleared my throat. "Maybe I'm a little anxious."

His grip increased on my hand as well. "I can take you back. You don't have to be here at all. We can leave."

I shook my head. "I have to talk to my aunt."

Then I froze as I heard a bellowing roar reverberate through the castle. The sound made me go cold with fear.

"What was *that*?" I managed.

Michael's arm came around my waist. "It's okay."

"It didn't sound okay. What was it?"

His jaw was tight. "Your father."

My heart clenched. My father made that horrible noise? It sounded like a creature in such anguish that death would be a relief.

"Don't cry," Michael said as he stroked my tears away.

"How can I not cry when my father is in so much pain?"

He swallowed. "Come on. Let's see your aunt."

I listened for any more sounds from my father, but there was only silence. We continued on through the castle until we came to an open doorway. I peered inside to see my aunt standing behind a black, marble-footed basin that looked like a very shallow freestanding sink. She stared down into the water as if mesmerized by what she saw there.

"What is she doing?" I whispered to Michael.

Elizabeth raised her head and looked directly at me. Her eyes were demon red, but then faded quickly to a hazel that matched my own. She smiled warmly at me.

"This is my gazer," she said. "I can use it as a communication device as long as whoever I'm trying to contact also has one."

"Like a two-way videophone?"

Her smile widened. "Yes, I'm sure it's very much like that."

She moved away from the basin so I could see that she wore a red dress with long, draping sleeves and gold flowers embroidered at the edges. It was low cut and the material split at the waist to show a black skirt beneath. Her blonde hair was in one thick braid that draped over her left shoulder. She still wore the small blue bottle of perfume from her boyfriend around her neck on a thin gold chain.

"Nikki," she said. "I didn't think I'd ever see you again. I'm so glad Michael has brought you back to see me."

"I'm glad to see you, too."

She approached me to give me a hug and then leaned back to look at me. "Although I'm worried. This means you haven't drunk your potion yet?"

"That's right."

Her forehead furrowed. "What does this mean?"

"It means that I wanted to see you again. And I want to

see my father before . . . before it's too late." I glanced at Michael, who had slunk back into the shadows at the side of the room and seemed to be studying the floor. "I heard him a minute ago."

"He's gotten much worse, I'm afraid."

"Michael told me there are only hours left. Do you really think so?"

She reached out to squeeze my hand. "It must be terrible for you. To find your father after all this time and then to have him taken from you in such a tragic way."

My throat thickened. "It *is* terrible."

"I think it's good that you've returned. We must cherish the short time we'll have together. I'll take you to see him if you like."

"As soon as possible."

"Of course." She nodded. "Nikki . . . did you happen to bring the potion with you or did you leave it at your home?"

"I have the bottle here." I unzipped my purse and pulled it out to show her. Then, instead of putting it back, I slid the chain over my head and let it drop to my chest.

"Did Desmond tell you that's all the potion there is?" she asked. "Such a small amount for such an important task. It's crucial that you keep it safe."

"He mentioned something like that." I traced my fingertip over the cool vial filled with red liquid, her words making me very nervous. *All there is.* "But can more be made if necessary?"

"Yes. It's possible, but difficult and time consuming."

She smiled. "It helps the potion makers to command a high price in return for their skills. Supply and demand."

"Can I ask you a hypothetical question that I've been wondering about?" I asked.

"Of course."

"Okay, so let's say somebody drinks a potion, but then something bad happens and they change their mind. Could it be reversed? Is there, like, *another* potion they could take to cancel out the effects?"

She looked at me with confusion. "Why would that be something you're concerned with?"

"I don't know." I crossed my arms, the whole situation making every muscle in my body tense. "I've been working out all sorts of ideas. I was thinking earlier, what if I drank the potion, waited long enough for you to become queen, and then, if there's a reversal potion, I could drink that so I could remember everything?" I stopped talking and chewed my bottom lip nervously.

"Oh, Nikki." She touched my face. "That is a very clever idea. Yes, the Underworld potion makers always create an anti-potion for everything. It's a by-product of the potion itself and a very good fail-safe—after all, one can never be too careful when it comes to magical brews."

"It's like an antidote?"

"Yes. But I don't think it'll work," Elizabeth continued. "I'd love for you to keep your memories. I'd love to get to know you and have you visit me once I'm unable to leave the castle. But I'm worried it won't work as well as you think it will."

"Why not?" I asked. I'd already assumed that particular idea of mine might not work, but I was still disappointed it was getting shot down so quickly by my aunt.

"Along with your memories come the problems we had to begin with. The deadly instability of your Darkling status, for one. I've already told you of the poor creatures in the past who've died from harnessing their powers. And also, there is no guarantee that once you drink the anti-potion, the power of the kingdom won't then shift to you, when it realizes that you are again half demon. Your safety is my first concern."

I touched the vial at the end of my chain. "I appreci-ate that. But maybe I'm different. It's been a long time since the last Darkling."

"Perhaps. But it's too dangerous to take that risk," she said. "You really must drink the potion now."

"I need to see my father first."

She squeezed my hand. "I'll take you when I check in on him shortly. He's sent all of the servants away, now. He doesn't want anyone to see him as he is, but I'm sure he'll make an exception for you."

I swallowed hard, relieved that she didn't want to keep arguing with me about the potion or seeing my father in his current condition. "Thank you."

I wanted to tell her about turning Darkling and being okay, but I decided to listen to Michael. Not yet. She would be more worried than she already was.

I glanced over at her gazer. "Who were you talking to before I got here?"

"My boyfriend. Or rather"—she frowned—"I was *trying* to speak with him, but I couldn't seem to make contact."

"You mentioned him yesterday," I said. "Who is he?"

Maybe it was none of my business, but I was curious. My aunt was still a complete mystery to me. She was beautiful and kind and concerned for my well-being even though she hadn't known I existed until just the other day. She was willing to sacrifice her freedom to become queen here in this empty castle. It seemed like a huge sacrifice to me.

"He's one of the princes of the Underworld—the opposite side to where we are now. His name is Kieran." She smiled then. "He's wonderful, really. So very handsome. I would have loved for you to meet him."

That's where my father had said there were dragons. I still couldn't believe all of these other worlds existed alongside mine and I'd never had any idea.

"I lived there for several years until recently. I wanted to spend more time with Desmond so I returned here. I knew my brother was very lonely."

I thought of how isolated my father must have been over the years. "Was there ever a queen? Did my father ever fall in love with anyone else?"

She shook her head. "Desmond has been devoted to the Shadowlands and protecting the human and faery realms. I suggested that a queen could be found for him, but he refused." She sighed. "I'm afraid he never moved on after your mother."

"He thought she was dead. All of those years."

"He loved her very much." She glanced at her gazer.

"Like I love Kieran. I miss him already. I hope that he'll come to visit me very soon."

"So he'll be able to come here?" I asked. "I know my father said that other demons can't enter the Shadowlands."

"They can't," she said. "Not without the king's permission. Or with *my* permission soon, I suppose. I will make an exception for Kieran, of course."

"Of course."

"Do you have a boyfriend, Nikki?"

That was a question I didn't really know how to answer. A couple days ago I would have said it was Chris, and that I was so happy about it, but now everything had changed. Drastically.

I forced myself not to glance at Michael, who stood silently behind me, but I could feel him looking at me.

::Well, Princess? Are you going to answer her question?::

I was glad he didn't use that ability of his too much. It was very distracting.

What do you think I should tell her? I projected back to him telepathically.

::Whatever you wish.::

I shifted my weight to my right bare foot. "There's somebody I'm interested in . . . but it's kind of complicated."

Her lips stretched into a small grin. "Love is always complicated, Nikki. What is this somebody like?"

Tall, dark, totally hot, and standing right behind me, I thought. However, I didn't send that particular thought to Michael.

Instead, I shrugged. "He's really cute, even though he

tries to hide it. He can be annoying and stubborn but that's just part of his charm. He's protective and sweet and an amazing kisser, and when I'm around him I don't want to be anywhere else."

She looked very impressed by my description. "He sounds perfect to me."

"The thing is," I continued, "I'm not totally sure how he feels about me. Sometimes I get the feeling that he wants me to forget him, like, maybe his life would be easier if I wasn't in it. And then other times I feel like he thinks he's not good enough for me because we're really different in a lot of ways. The guy is a serious mystery."

"Well, that's *not* perfect." Elizabeth took my hands in hers. "Nikki, dear, don't let anyone hold you back from getting what you want. Sometimes you have to trust your heart. Trust what that little voice inside is trying to tell you, even if it seems crazy."

I let out a shaky breath. "It's hard to do that."

"I know it is. But that's my philosophy, and I've held on to it, no matter what difficult choices I've had to make."

"That's great."

She smiled. "Love is the most important thing in the universe. Like how I love Kieran and how I love my brother. Desmond should have lived for many more years to rule the Shadowlands, but when he asked me to take over for him, I knew I'd never turn my back on such an important duty. Even if it means sacrificing many things. I will make sure I'm a very good queen—for my brother's sake."

My eyes welled with tears. "You'll make a great queen."

She stroked my arm. "We should go see your father now."

I nodded. "Okay."

She glanced at Michael. "Would you please go to Desmond's side and inform him that his daughter wishes to see him one last time?"

"Of course," Michael said.

::Will you be all right, Princess?::

Yeah, I'll be fine, I thought.

There was a hesitation. ::I *don't* want you to forget me. I just wish there was another way this could work out.::

Our eyes met and held for a long moment, then he turned and left the room.

16

After Michael left, Elizabeth looked at me with concern as my eyes filled up with tears again. I didn't think I'd cried so much in my entire life as I had over the last two days. "Oh, Nikki, my dear. So much stress at such a young age. Is it too much for you?"

"I'll be fine," I said shakily as I twisted my bracelet.

Elizabeth looked down at it. "That's very beautiful."

I looked down at it, too. "My father gave it to me. It's a dragon's tear. He told me it would help focus my Darkling powers."

"A dragon's tear? He told you that?"

I nodded.

Her expression grew tense. "I'm sorry, Nikki. The pain he is feeling must be making him delusional. There are no dragons—they are only a myth." She looked thoughtful. "Our father used to tell us stories about dragons when we were young so perhaps that's what Desmond is remembering. It's a lovely bracelet, but that's all it is."

I studied the delicate chain and teardrop crystal and felt a stab of disappointment. "Really?"

"I'm afraid so." She walked to the entrance of the room. "Now I must go get some fresh water for Desmond. It's all he's been able to consume for days. No wonder he's so weak." She shook her head sadly. "I'll return to bring you to his room. Please wait here for me."

She left and I was all alone. I crossed my arms and tried to relax but found that it was impossible. So instead I began to pace back and forth across the cool stone floor.

I couldn't believe that nothing could be done for my father. This was the best he could ask for? Being stuck in this dreary castle as the last hours of his life ticked by? What about doctors? Or hospitals? But I supposed those were out of the question anyway, since he couldn't leave. I still couldn't fathom being trapped inside this place for all those years. Alone. At least he had Elizabeth to keep him company in these dark days.

I heard something then.

"Elizabeth?" an unfamiliar voice said. I looked around the room but there was no one there.

I heard it again. A deep voice calling out for my aunt. I walked toward the gazer and looked down at the shallow black water. I gasped when I saw a face looking up at me. The image of a man appeared on the surface of the water. It rippled when I clutched the sides of the basin.

He raised an eyebrow. "You're not Elizabeth."

I swallowed hard. "No."

"Who are you?"

"I'm . . . I'm Nikki."

Both of his dark eyebrows went up at that. "Ah, *Princess*

Nikki. I've heard a great deal about you. It's a pleasure to meet you, even if it's not in person. My name is Kieran."

It was Elizabeth's boyfriend—the demon prince from the Underworld, though he was definitely in human form. He looked a lot like the male model on the front of my mom's vampire romance book—dark hair, cool blue eyes, and strongly handsome features. He was so acutely good-looking that it seemed vaguely artificial, as if he were made of plastic—his eyes were so ice-blue that they gave me an immediate chill. His too-full lips curled to one side as he gazed up at me.

I looked toward the entrance of the room. "Elizabeth just left. But she was waiting for your . . . uh . . . your *call.* I'll go get her."

"No, Nikki. It's fine. I will speak with her later. How is your father?"

I swallowed. "Not well."

"But he still lives?"

I nodded.

"Elizabeth tells me that you were to drink a potion that the king provided to you. I will assume that you haven't yet."

I touched the bottle. "No, I haven't."

"Do you *want* to be queen of the Shadowlands?" he asked.

I shook my head. "Not if I can help it."

"Then you have to drink it."

There was that phrase again. *Have to.* Even somebody I didn't know was telling me what to do.

I let out a shaky sigh. "I wanted to see my father again before I do anything."

Something flashed behind his eyes and it wasn't entirely pleasant. "You do realize that you're putting Elizabeth's position as the next queen at risk by delaying."

"Look," I said, sharper than I meant to, "this isn't exactly easy for me, you know. And it's not easy for Elizabeth, either. It's not like she even wants to be queen."

His eyes widened a fraction. "Of course she does. It's all she speaks of and your actions—or rather *inactions*—are ruining everything for her."

That was a very strange thing for him to say. I was *ruining* everything? "She's accepted it, of course. It's not like she has much of a choice, does she?"

"No, of course. You're right. Please forgive me for being rude. The choice is yours alone, of course." The edge of annoyance in his expression disappeared and his gaze slowly moved over my face and down my neck to the vial on the chain. "If by chance you do end up becoming queen, I want you to know that you can contact me anytime. For any reason at all. I would enjoy the chance to get to know a lovely girl like yourself on a much more personal level. I'm sure we could become very close friends."

The way he said it made me feel extremely uncomfortable. This was the man my aunt was head over heels in love with? He was a major sleaze. Really good-looking, but a jerk. I knew I'd just met him, but first impressions were enough to go by.

Besides, I'd already dealt with a good-looking jerk that evening—Chris—so I was a little more wary of this sort of thing now. I trusted my instincts. And my instincts told me Kieran wasn't a nice guy.

"I'll keep that in mind," I said dryly.

"However, if Elizabeth *does* become queen of the Shadowlands, I would like to give her a little something special to . . . *commemorate* this event. Do you have any suggestions for me? Perhaps jewels, or furs. More obedient servants, perhaps?"

I really didn't like this guy. *At all.*

"I know she likes the perfume you already gave her," I said with distaste. "She even wears the bottle on a chain around her neck."

"Perfume?" His frown deepened and confusion flashed across his expression. "I've never given her perfume before."

"Maybe I heard her wrong."

"No," he replied quickly. "If Elizabeth said I gave her the perfume, then I certainly did. I give her many gifts and I have a tendency to forget some of them."

He glanced over his shoulder at something I couldn't see. When he turned back, he said, "I must go now, Princess Nikki. Please tell Elizabeth that I wish to speak with her at her earliest convenience."

His image faded until there was nothing but shallow water in the basin.

Elizabeth had said that she received her perfume from her boyfriend. Had Kieran really forgotten? Maybe she had more than one boyfriend? She was a beautiful woman, so it was entirely possible. I hoped I hadn't ruined anything by mentioning it to Kieran.

Then again, after my very short conversation with the handsome Kieran, I figured Elizabeth would be better off without him. I did *not* like the way he leered at me. I mean, the guy had to be at least thirty years old—and that was assuming that demons aged at the same rate humans did.

Creepy.

And what was all that about Elizabeth *wanting* to be queen? I mean, I understood that she'd accepted the inevitable, but the way Kieran said it, it sounded like she was actually looking forward to it. What was that all about?

I started to wonder what was taking Elizabeth so long, so I left the room to look for her, feeling uncomfortable being in the room with the gazer any longer. I headed along the hallway to the end where it turned to the right and kept following it until I saw Elizabeth go into a room up ahead. When I got to the doorway, I saw that she had a tray with a jug of water and a silver goblet. She poured a few drops from her small perfume bottle into the jug and then stirred the contents with a large silver-handled spoon.

"Elizabeth?" I said out loud.

She turned to look at me with wide eyes. "Nikki! You startled me."

"Sorry."

"I was about to come back for you."

"What is that?" I asked, pointing at the jug. "I thought that was perfume you wore around your neck."

She touched the blue bottle and I noticed her hand was shaking a little. "This . . . no, this is medicine. It's to help with Desmond's pain. A few drops will ease his suffering. My perfume is in another bottle." She smiled. "They all look very similar, don't they?"

I studied the vial skeptically. They did look similar. *Really* similar. "Could be Gatorade for all I know."

She tilted her head to the side. "What is Gatorade?"

"It's a drink. You can get it in the blue flavor if you want."

She smiled. "The human world is a fascinating place, isn't it?"

"Depends on the day, really."

"Indeed." She picked up the tray. "I'm ready. We can go see your father now if you wish."

I swallowed. "Okay."

She left the room. I followed her through the mazelike hallways. I braced myself to hear another cry of pain, but there was only silence.

I tried to remain calm and not overthink things, but my brief conversation with Kieran had deeply confused me. I had a hard time concentrating on anything else.

"I have never given her perfume before."

It was probably nothing, of course. It was also probably nothing that Elizabeth's perfume vial looked exactly the same as the container of my father's pain meds. My aunt was a kind woman who was looking after her dying brother. She was sacrificing her freedom to become queen because she felt it was her duty. She didn't even *want* to be queen.

Who would want to be trapped in this castle without the opportunity of leaving?

But still. Something felt off to me.

"It's all she speaks of." Kieran's words echoed in my mind.

"Desmond," my aunt said as she entered my father's room. Michael stood at the far side against the wall, silent. He looked at me and he smiled a little—just enough for me to see. "Nikki is here with me."

"Yes," a deep voice replied. "I sensed that she had returned."

My father, in full demon form, lay on a huge canopied bed in the middle of the room. He raised his head a little to look at me and I saw his eyes flash red.

"Nikki." His voice was weak. "You shouldn't have returned. I didn't want you to see me like this again. Please don't be afraid."

My heart clenched and I went directly to his side. This time, unlike last night when his demon form had taken me by surprise and scared me deeply, I could see him more clearly. He had coal black skin and a ridged forehead with large, curved horns protruding from his temples. His cheek-bones and chin were sharp and angular. The tips of his ears came to a point and his eyes were catlike and glowed with dull red light in the dimness of the room.

The room was a bit different from the others I'd seen. While I could tell that it still had black stone walls and floors, it had a few more personal touches. Colorful draperies and beautifully detailed paintings covered the walls. The scenes depicted seemed to be those of my world: waterfalls, sunsets, and beautiful meadows. In a frame among the other paintings there was an oil painting of a smiling woman who looked remarkably like my mother. It was dim in there, lit by a few torches.

My father was covered by a blanket, but his large, heavily muscled bare arms lay on top. The skin looked leathery, similar to the wings that extended from his back, folded in on themselves so I could barely see them now. His hands were clenched over his stomach as if he expected to be racked with pain at any moment.

I wanted to tell him about my Darkling form. How I'd shifted completely and was still okay. How maybe I was the exception—that maybe I wasn't at risk of dying early like the others had. But I still didn't know for sure. I didn't want to worry him or Elizabeth, so I held my tongue.

Elizabeth, who wanted to take the throne. According to her boyfriend, that is.

I reached out and put my hand on top of my father's, and the skin did feel leathery, but smooth and warm. He looked up at me with surprise.

"I had to see you again," I said.

"Why?" he asked hoarsely.

"Because you're my father."

His currently hairless brows drew together. "Nikki . . . you have to go home and be happy. Be with your mother. Take care of her for me. Please forget about all of this. It's for the best."

"Your father is right," Elizabeth said.

Her voice made me tense.

I watched her warily as she put the tray on a bedside table and then poured water mixed with the medicine into the goblet and brought it to my father's lips. "Drink this, Desmond. It will help."

He did. I waited for her to mention the medicine, but she didn't say a word. My father didn't give any indication that he tasted anything other than water.

Did he know that there was pain medication in his water? She'd been taking care of him for a while, so I guessed it would be expected.

But why had she jumped when I caught her mixing it into the water earlier? Why had her hand been shaking?

"Thank you," he said when he was done. "I'm so lucky to have had you near me ever since this horrible illness began, Elizabeth."

She stroked his forehead. "I wouldn't have it any other way."

"Elizabeth returned to the castle before you got sick?" I asked.

"Yes," my father said. "I don't know what I would have done without her."

Elizabeth squeezed his hand. "I only wish I could ease your pain, brother."

His attention returned to me and he looked at the vial I wore on the chain around my neck. "Why haven't you drunk the potion yet? I thought it was what you wanted."

"I wanted to see you again."

He managed a very small smile at that. "Even when I'm stuck in this form?"

I nodded. His demon form was a fearsome thing, and at first glance anyone would assume that he was a monster, but I now knew that he wasn't. As he'd said to me yesterday, he was the same man underneath, no matter what outer form he took. I had no doubt that my father was a good man, even though he was also a demon.

It sounded completely crazy, but I believed it.

I wasn't afraid of him. I hadn't known him for my entire life, but I knew at that moment that I loved him. I loved my father so much and I didn't want him to die.

My eyes burned with tears. I'd seen him one last time. I'd done what I wanted. I'd shown him that I wasn't afraid of him—I didn't want the last time he saw me to have been last night when I screamed because I was afraid of how he looked.

Now the only thing I was afraid of was losing him before I got the chance to even get to know him.

I cleared my throat and looked around the room. "The pictures. Where did you get them?"

"I painted them myself. My memories of being in the human realm are still very vivid. I wanted to remember what I'd seen."

"And the one of my mother?"

"I painted that one as well." His eyes moved to it. "I can still see her when I close my eyes, as if I was with her only yesterday."

Just then, his face convulsed and he clutched at his stomach. The veins and muscles in his neck bulged. He was in pain but wasn't crying out this time. Was it because I was in the room next to him? Did he not want me to see how much agony he was in? Was he holding in the scream so it wouldn't scare me? I felt like sobbing for him, for his pain, and for everything he was going through.

Why wasn't the pain medication Elizabeth gave him working? Was it too late?

When he settled down he met my gaze again. "I'm sorry, Nikki," his voice rasped. "For all of this."

I shook my head and clutched on to his hand tighter. "Don't be sorry."

He turned to Elizabeth. "May I have some more water?"

"Of course." She poured more and brought it to him again, holding it up so he could drink. He was so weak he could barely swallow.

I knew then that Elizabeth was right. He had only hours left. Perhaps not even that long.

Michael's expression was tense. "I'll get more water."

"No, I will." Elizabeth absently touched the small bottle she wore around her neck and I took a good, close look at it.

It *was* the same bottle as yesterday. I was sure of it. Why would perfume and pain medicine be in the exact same bottle? Why would they be the exact same color?

My thoughts churned together in a big confusing mass as I tried to make sense of everything I'd seen and heard. It felt like there was an answer there—something I was missing. Something that would make sense of everything.

Michael, I projected telepathically. *Does my aunt control everything that my father drinks or eats?*

There was a pause. ::As far as I know. After she sent the rest of the servants away, no one else was here to do it. And she doesn't let me do anything.::

She sent the servants away? She told me that my father did that.

::No, it was her decision. I was only able to stay because the king insisted.::

Does she have another boyfriend or is it just the prince from the Underworld?

::It's just him. She's very devoted to him. I'm surprised she even came back to the castle since she had to leave his side to return.::

It was right before my father got sick?

::Yes, that's right.::

My aunt turned to me then and gave me a kind smile. "I must go get more water. Have a few more minutes with your father, but then he needs his rest. Before you leave, however, I must insist that you drink the potion. As you have seen for yourself, there is no other solution to this unfortunate situation. I will have to take the burden of becoming queen. There is no other choice."

I nodded and watched as she took the tray and left the room. My father closed his eyes and I watched him, sensing how close he now was to the end.

My head was spinning, my brain swarming with information that I knew was important but that I couldn't quite piece together. Things that Kieran had told me only added to my confusion.

He made it sound as if Elizabeth wanted to be queen

more than anything, but she'd told me she was only doing it out of duty. That it was, as she'd just said, a *burden*.

He hadn't given her perfume even though she said it was a gift from him. And now what I thought was a perfume bottle held medicine that she mixed into my father's drinking water.

My aunt had returned to live at the castle, leaving the man she said she was in love with, just before my father became sick.

I started breathing very fast then as it all began to click into place and my heart pounded twice as quickly in my chest.

Michael, I thought and turned to look at him. *Michael . . . I don't think my father is really sick. I don't think he's got an illness at all.*

::What do you mean?::

He's . . . he's not sick. It's Elizabeth. She wants to be queen. She wants me to drink the potion so I don't get in the way of her taking the throne. That has to be it. It has to be.

He frowned at me. ::Nikki—::

Oh, my God, Michael. She hasn't been giving him medicine, has she? It's poison. Elizabeth has been poisoning him slowly, hasn't she? He isn't dying at all. He's being murdered!

Panic clutched at my throat. I had to be wrong. She couldn't do something like this to her own brother, could she? It was impossible.

Michael didn't think anything for a very long time and I looked at him and waited, wanting him to tell me I was crazy, that I was overreacting, that I was grasping at straws and seeing clues when there were none. His expression was unreadable. And then in the back of my mind, I heard him project two small words that changed everything for me right then and there.

::You're right.::

17

I was stunned.

How do you know? I thought frantically. *Why didn't you tell me?*

But before he could answer me, Elizabeth returned to place the tray next to my father's bed. Her hand curled around my shoulder.

"It's time, Nikki." She glanced down at my father. "He's sleeping now. He falls in and out of consciousness. It makes it easier for him that way."

I just stared at her.

Then I heard Michael's voice in my head.

::Nikki, say nothing. Don't let on that you know anything. *Please*, trust me.::

"This . . ." I tried to breathe normally. "This has been very difficult."

She shook her head. "Did I mention how beautiful you look today? That dress is lovely."

"I . . . I was at a dance before I came here."

"And that's how it should be. Sixteen-year-old girls shouldn't have to worry about these sorts of things. You should think about dances, and friends, and boys. It'll be fine, soon. Everything will be back to how it was meant to be. I promise you."

I just looked at her. How could she seem so nice, even now? Even when I knew the horrible truth? Maybe I was wrong, maybe Michael was wrong.

But no. It was true. I felt it deep inside of me.

"You said that Darklings die before they're eighteen," I said quietly. "But you didn't say *how* they die."

"That part of history is quite vague. I searched for as much as I could find, but the details are sketchy. I would assume that their hearts stopped working during their change to Darkling form. Or perhaps their poor little bodies simply gave out. It's impossible to expect human and demon forms to blend together. It's like oil and water. They can't be combined."

"But are you just guessing that, or do you know for sure?"

The edge of Elizabeth's mouth tightened almost imperceptibly. "For something that happened so long ago, it's difficult to say for sure, of course."

I looked down at my father. My hand hadn't left his for the whole time I'd been in the room and now I clung to him like I would never let go.

Did he have any idea what his sister was doing to him? He shielded the human and faery realms from anything that might do them harm, stopping evil from crossing the Shadowlands, but he had no idea that evil was already there. He protected everybody, but nobody had protected him.

Elizabeth pulled me away from my father's unconscious form and hugged me tightly. "It's good that he's sleeping now. I fear that Desmond will be in horrible pain right until the end, just like our father was. My only solace is that the end is very close now."

Had she poisoned her father, too? If this was the same way her father had died, the similarities seemed too coincidental.

She took my hand in hers and brought me over to the entrance. "He's been so strong. He's fought to live, Nikki, and I think a great part of that was learning of your existence. My father passed on much quicker. Desmond is strong, though—he's a fighter. But fighting is only prolonging his suffering. He needs to let go now, and I think that when you drink the potion, he'll be able to."

"Where do demons go when they die?" I asked, trying to stall for time. Trying to figure out what to do next.

"Where do we go?" she repeated. "We are not like humans. We have no immortal soul that must be divvied up between Heaven and Hell. All the more reason we should never coexist or fall in love with humans, you see. When a demon dies or is vanquished, we are gone. We refer to it as the Void—our place of eternal rest."

Elizabeth looked over at Michael then. "Please take Nikki downstairs," she said. "I must stay with my brother to see if he needs anything. He isn't usually asleep for long periods. I will join you momentarily." She turned back to me and took my cold, clammy hand in her warm, dry one and squeezed it gently. "Then you'll drink the potion and Michael will take you home. Does that sound acceptable to you?"

I nodded stiffly. Michael came to my side and our eyes met for a moment before he looked away.

As I took a last glance at my father, I felt Michael's fingers close around my wrist and he began walking me away from the room.

"Oh, I almost forgot," I called back to Elizabeth. "Your boyfriend showed up on your gazer after you left."

"He did?" She looked surprised. "What did he say?"

"Lots of things," I replied, just before Michael and I disappeared around a corner.

He picked up his pace, my hand now in his iron vise of a grip.

"I never should have brought you back," he said. "I'm so stupid."

"So it's true? It's all true? Elizabeth is—"

"Shh, not here. It's too dangerous."

We reached the spiral staircase and began to descend it so quickly I nearly slipped a few times. When we finally got to the bottom, Michael pulled me right toward the front doors, which immediately opened for me. I picked up my shoes from where I'd left them for safekeeping.

"Michael, talk to me." My voice shook. "Are you in on this? Are you helping Elizabeth kill my father?"

I still couldn't believe what I was saying. Finding out my father was dying was one thing. But poisoned? It was too horrible to contemplate.

He stopped walking and spun around to face me, the expression on his face distraught. "Of course not."

"Then how do you know?"

"I've been suspicious of her motives for some time and you just confirmed it for me. When I came back last night after seeing you home, she asked me questions about you. She wanted to know everything. She wanted to know if you'd drunk the potion and I told her you weren't ready yet. She wasn't happy about that. I didn't know why, but the way she was acting was very telling. When I guessed, she nearly . . ." He blinked. "She nearly killed me right then and there. But she didn't."

I could barely breathe. "Michael—did she hurt you?"

He shook his head. "No, but I wouldn't put it past her." He grabbed my hand and pulled me around to the right side of the castle, away from view. "You need to leave. Right now. You need to go back home. Drink the potion. It's the only way you'll be safe."

My head was spinning. "I can't do that."

"She might not look like it, but Elizabeth is very worried about you, and not in a caring-aunt kind of way. She is afraid that you won't drink the potion and when the king dies you'll become queen and ruin her plans."

"But I don't understand. What are her plans? She'll be trapped in the castle when she's queen."

"It's Kieran. Elizabeth has always wanted power, but he's the one who's in charge. He's convinced her that now is the time to completely join the Shadowlands with the

Underworld. Because she loves him, he'll be able to manip-ulate her. He'll control the barrier that separates Hell and the Underworld from the faery and human realms."

I put a hand over my mouth in shock. "And my father has no idea?"

"She puts on a good act. She's probably been putting on the same act her entire life. She fooled me. She fooled you. She comes across as so nice but she isn't, Princess."

I thought about how I'd also been fooled by Chris, who seemed so popular and great to be around, until he attacked me in the back of a limo.

Appearance means nothing. It only hides what's underneath—be it good or bad.

I blinked slowly. "She's the one who sent the guy with the knife after me, isn't she?"

He nodded. "She isn't playing games. When the king found out about you, he was very happy to learn he had a daughter. She pretended to be, but I could see that she wasn't. I couldn't imagine why at the time . . ."

"She prevented you from coming to see me today, didn't she? That's why you weren't around earlier?"

He nodded again. "She wouldn't let me leave. The king is weakened, so she was able to steal some of the kingdom's energy to let her thug come after you. Twice now." His jaw tightened. "When he failed, she allowed me to see you. To try to convince you to drink the potion once and for all. And if I failed . . ." He swallowed hard. "She wanted *me* to kill you."

My eyes widened at that. *"What?"*

"I wouldn't do it. I'd never hurt you, Princess. But I knew I had to make her think I was willing. It's the only way I could protect you. Then when you wanted to come here again . . ." He rubbed his mouth with the back of his hand, his face haunted. "I couldn't refuse you. But I thought maybe if you were here and drank the potion in front of her, then she'd know for sure. You'd have your peace of mind at seeing your father again, and Elizabeth would have her proof that you weren't trying to stop her. If I told you, I would have been putting you into even more danger. You never should have figured it out." He touched my face then. "You need to leave. It won't be long before she realizes you're not downstairs waiting for her."

"Why didn't she just try to kill me when we were alone upstairs?"

"The moment you returned to the Shadowlands, the king would have sensed your presence. He'd know if she killed you here, so that's stopping her. She's still uncertain how weak the king is. He's incredibly powerful when he's at full strength—much more powerful than she is. If he had the slightest inkling that she would hurt you, he would be furious."

I tried to think clearly but it was a struggle. "Elizabeth . . . she said that for every potion they make in the Underworld, they make an antidote. Do you think there might be an antidote for the poison?"

He shook his head. "I don't know. But there's no time for that. Princess, you have to go *now*."

"I can't leave my father. I can't leave you."

"You have to."

Have to.

I grabbed my potion bottle and squeezed. "I don't have to do anything if I don't want to."

"Princess, now is seriously not the time to be stubborn." His expression softened as he looked into my eyes. We were talking so closely that we were nearly hugging. His arms were around my waist.

The castle doors opened up again and Michael moved a bit so he could look around the corner. When he turned back to me his expression was even more tense than before. "It's Elizabeth's thug."

"The one who tried to kill me?"

He nodded. "She's sent him to find you. She must know you've already left the castle." He pulled off his sweatshirt and wrapped it around my shoulders to keep me warm. "Go. Run to the clearing and go through the gateway. I'll hold him off for as long as I can."

"He's going to hurt you."

He touched his amulet. "Not if I hurt him first."

"Michael . . . you can't—"

"Am I interrupting?" a deep voice asked.

I slowly looked to the side to see the brute standing there, a smile curling up the corners of his mouth.

"Princess," he said, "it's time for you to come back inside. Elizabeth wishes to talk with you."

"Just talk, huh?" I could barely breathe.

He grabbed for my arm but Michael pulled him away

from me and pushed him up against the wall. The brute backhanded Michael across his face and he went spinning, but the moment the creep came at me again Michael grabbed him hard around his neck.

"*Nikki!*" He used my real name then. "Go now. There's no time. Run!"

The thug was fighting to get Michael off him, and since he outweighed Michael by at least sixty pounds it wouldn't take long.

"Just go!" Michael yelled at me and his words finally broke through my shock.

Elizabeth wanted me dead. She'd poisoned her brother, more than likely her father as well, and I was the last thing standing in the way of what she wanted.

Fear trumped anger this time and, with a sob, I turned away from the castle and ran as fast as I could.

I ran until my bare feet began to bleed from stepping on the rocks; until I felt the cool grass under my feet and the temperature immediately warmed up as if by magic. I held my shoes by their straps in one hand and my little purse in the other and I ran faster than I'd ever run before. I tried not to think of Michael fighting to give me a chance to escape, but it was impossible. I had to get home where I could hide. I'd figure out what I had to do next once I was there.

"Stop!" A deep voice bellowed from behind me and I took a quick peek over my shoulder. It was the thug and he was running after me. What had happened to Michael? My heart twisted and I nearly tripped from losing my concentration. But I kept running.

The gateway shimmered and swirled its kaleidoscope of color as I made a beeline toward it, my heart drumming wildly in my chest.

But just before I reached it, the gateway . . . disappeared.

18

One moment my escape route to the human realm was there in front of me and the next it was gone. I skidded to a halt, craning my neck from side to side, looking all around the grassy clearing.

Where did it go? How was I supposed to get back home without it?

I couldn't, that's how. It was impossible.

Elizabeth's henchman was still thundering across the field toward me and I only had a split second to figure out what I was going to do next.

Panic shot through my entire body and my head screamed out in pain. I welcomed it this time, though. Maybe I could bring out my Darkling. The creep hadn't fared so well against demon-me before.

But nothing happened. No sparkling sensations under my skin. No energy balls to throw to protect myself. No horns. Just plain old Nikki Donovan, barefoot, wearing Michael's dark blue sweatshirt over my borrowed lavender designer dress.

I didn't have time to think about why the gateway wasn't working, so instead, I did the only thing I could do.

I ran toward the forest leading to the faery realm.

The darkness enveloped me as I ran past the tree line and into the thick foliage. I ducked behind a tree and peered around the massive, green, mossy trunk. The demon thug, with knife in hand, had stopped at the clearing well before the forest and was now staring into it. He backed up a few feet. I waited, holding my breath.

Would I be able to hide in here? And for how long?

He didn't do anything for a few minutes except look at the forest, attempting to peer inside.

Why wasn't he chasing me in here?

I kept waiting, barely breathing, for a few more minutes, wondering desperately what he was going to do next. He looked confused, his large Neanderthal-like forehead creased in concentration. He rubbed a hand over his stubble-covered head.

Go away, I thought fiercely. *Leave me alone.*

Then, as if he'd heard my thoughts as readily as Michael could pick up my telepathy, he turned around and began walking back toward the castle.

I let out a deep breath I hadn't even realized I'd been holding. My hands were shaking so badly I had to press them against my sides or I'd end up dropping my shoes and purse. I closed my eyes and tried to calm down, but that seemed like an impossibility.

Everything had gone wrong. Why did I ask to come

back to the Shadowlands? I should have just drunk the potion yesterday as soon as I'd gotten it, and then none of this would have happened.

But, no. That wasn't right, either. I would have been safe and I would have forgotten all about this, but it wouldn't have changed much. My father would still be poisoned and on the verge of death. My aunt would still be scheming to become queen, and what impact would that have on the worlds the Shadowlands protected in the first place? And Michael . . .

Michael.

Was he okay? I wondered if that creep had hurt him or if he had managed to use his amulet for protection. And if so, had he used up all his power? Was he unconscious somewhere and completely helpless?

Michael! I channeled my thoughts telepathically. *Are you there? Can you hear me?*

There was no reply, only silence.

Could I turn Darkling if I focused hard enough? Even if I wasn't experiencing high emotion? Could I *make* myself change?

I thought about trying it but stopped myself. When I'd changed before, I'd only been in half-demon form for a few minutes before I shifted back to normal. That wouldn't even be enough time to get back to the castle, let alone try to help anyone. And besides, just because Elizabeth was evil didn't mean that she'd been lying when she'd told me about Darklings dying from using their abilities. It was still a risk I didn't want to take.

Not yet. Maybe soon, but not quite yet.

A sudden noise distracted me from my thoughts. There was a rustling sound close by. I tensed and listened hard, but there was nothing else.

Just my imagination.

Then I felt something warm nudge at my elbow and almost jumped right out of my skin. I looked down with horror, bracing myself for the worst, but then let out a long, shaky sigh of relief.

It was just a horse standing next to me in the lush forest backdrop.

A white horse. *Pure* white.

It looked slightly sparkly, actually.

And the sparkly white horse had a golden horn protruding from its forehead.

It wasn't a horse at all. I'd been nudged by a unicorn.

A freaking *unicorn*.

I stared at it dumbly. I'd never seen a unicorn before. Mainly because, along with demons and faeries, I didn't know they actually existed. After the experiences I'd had, I half-expected it to bare long, sharp fangs and try to attack me, but it didn't, so I studied it some more. It was absolutely beautiful—smaller than a regular horse, with a completely white coat and sky blue eyes. The spiraling horn looked as if it were made from pure gold.

"I suppose you're going to tell me that dragons really do exist, too," I said after another moment of stunned silence.

The unicorn didn't reply.

"You wouldn't happen to know where I can find a

gateway to the human realm around here, would you?" Maybe I'd gone a little crazy from all the panic and fear. I was probably headed into a new mental category altogether.

The unicorn moved away and began to graze on a patch of grass and blue flowers at the base of a tree. I looked around me for the first time. The forest was so thick I couldn't even see the sky. It felt like dusk in here, quiet and dark, and it smelled fresh and alive.

To the far side of the tree was a small creek that led deeper into the forest. The unicorn moved over there after nibbling on the grass for a moment and bent its head to drink. I walked over to the creek, watching where I stepped since I was still barefoot, and when the unicorn didn't run away I tucked my purse under my arm and stroked its pure white mane with a shaky hand.

"What am I going to do?" I asked, feeling tears getting ready to fall again.

"Unicorns don't talk, actually," a voice said and I froze in place. "And it's a bit late, but I should probably let you know it's against our laws for an outsider to touch one."

I turned slowly.

A guy leaned against the tree I'd hidden behind. At first glance I could tell he was very cute, with cropped chestnut brown hair and dark brown eyes. He wore tan-colored leather pants and a canvas tunic.

Tension flowed through my body again as I immediately put up my guard. "Who are you?"

He tilted his head as he took in the sight of me. "I was about to ask you the very same question."

"I'm Nikki." I held on to my shoes so tightly now that the straps were leaving a red imprint on my skin.

"I'm Rhys," he said. "Nikki, you look absolutely petrified."

He said it very coolly, very casually, but it didn't set me at ease. What did he want? What was he doing in the forest?

But he was correct. I *was* frozen in fear and that wasn't going to help at all. I forced myself to calm down.

The unicorn wandered away from the creek and deeper into the forest, apparently unaffected by the anxiety that must have been coming off me in waves.

"What are you doing here?" Rhys asked.

I glanced around. "I'm . . . I'm hiding from someone. I didn't have anywhere else to go."

His eyebrows raised. "Hiding from somebody who wants to hurt you?"

I nodded shakily. He studied me so intently I felt even more uncomfortable for a moment. But he didn't make any move to come closer to me; instead he stayed by the tree, leaning against it as if he were hanging out at the mall food court having a casual conversation with somebody passing by.

"I think I know who you are," he finally said. "It took me a minute, since you're better looking than I thought you'd be, but I think I've got it."

My cheeks flushed. "Look, Rhys, can you help me find a gateway to the human realm? I have to get to one so I can figure out what to do next."

"You're the princess, aren't you?" he asked.

I blinked at him.

"King Desmond's secret daughter," he clarified, as if I didn't know what he was talking about. "Gossip gets around quickly in these parts."

I nodded cautiously. "That's me. Who are you?"

He crossed his arms. "I already told you, I'm Rhys."

"Do you live here?"

"I do."

I looked around again. My feet were growing damp from standing on the cool mossy ground. "This is the faery realm?"

"That's right." He looked up at the tall, thick trees that surrounded us. "This forest is the very edge of its north border and the kingdom is several miles south. Nobody from the Shadowlands or beyond ever comes in here." He crossed his arms and smiled at me. "I'm actually very surprised to see that you did, especially considering who you are."

I craned my neck to peer through the thick trees and out to the clearing again. Maybe Rhys could help me. He studied me intently, as if he'd never seen a teenage girl up close and personal before. I guess I could work with that.

He was so relaxed and friendly that just being around him was beginning to put me a little more at ease. Not much, but a little.

"The guy who was chasing me seemed afraid to come in here," I said.

I remembered what Michael had told me about the faeries. How they were territorial and fierce, but not evil. I held on tightly to that thought.

"I imagine that he was afraid." Rhys stepped away from the tree and took a few steps closer to me, and then I could see his wings. Maybe it was because my head had been too filled with worries and stress to have clued into the truth yet.

I swallowed hard. "You're a faery?"

"Good guess."

His wings were very different from demons' wings. Where mine and my father's were black and leathery, Rhys's were fine and thin, white and delicate. Beautiful, really. Like something out of a fairy tale—which made a lot of sense, now that I thought about it. The surface of his wings glistened in the small amount of light filtering through the leaves above and showed different colors swirling around on the surface in an opalescent blend—pink, blue, green, purple.

"My realm is rarely bothered by unwanted visitors," Rhys said.

"*Your* realm?"

He casually ran a hand through his short brown hair. "I'm the king here."

My eyebrows went up. "You're the *king*? But you're so young."

"You're not the first person to say that." Rhys grinned. "Faeries are known to live for a very long time—hundreds of years, actually. But I'm only sixteen."

"Me, too."

I took another moment to look at him from hair to feet. He was barefoot just like I was. Other than the wings and the slightly pointed tips to his ears, he looked like a normal human teenager.

He laughed and turned around slowly. "Like what you see?"

My cheeks warmed again. "Look, Rhys, I have to go. I can't stay here any longer. Can you help me find a gateway to get home?"

He drew closer until he was only an arm's reach away. I watched him cautiously but didn't feel afraid of him anymore. He was even better-looking close up. He reminded me of Michael a bit with his earnest but guarded gaze. Michael wasn't quite so quick to flirt and joke around, though.

Rhys narrowed his eyes and peered at me. "You live in the human realm?"

"Uh . . . yeah."

"I've never visited there before. I've always wanted to."

"Look, I don't mean to be rude, but I'm in a lot of trouble. I have to—"

"Is it Elizabeth?" he asked. "She's responsible for all of this angst you're experiencing, isn't she?"

My eyes widened. "Do you know her?"

"She wants the throne. She's willing to do whatever it takes to get it." He took a lock of my hair between his fingers and studied it as if he'd never seen anything like it before. I inhaled sharply, but didn't move away from him. Then his brown eyes returned to mine. "I met her once and could easily sense the darkness she tries to hide. She's really quite horrible."

"She's poisoning my father. That's why he's dying. I have to stop her."

"Good plan." He cocked his head to the side and his

gaze moved down to my dress. He reached out to touch it and I finally backed away from him. He was very touchy-feely. "You're a Darkling. It's strange, but I can't even see much demon in you at all. I can sense it, but I can't see it. And I'm not sensing any darkness in you. I wonder why that is."

"Darkness?"

"Of course." He smiled, but continued to assess me as if I were on a slide under a microscope. "As I said, gossip travels fast around here. When word got out that King Desmond had a daughter—a Darkling—and that you were going to visit, my advisors and I were quite concerned."

"You were concerned about *me?*"

He nodded slowly. "Can't be too careful about these things. Especially if one takes the dangerous history of half-demon and half-human Darklings into consideration."

I felt like he was talking in circles and I was already dizzy to start with. I was wasting time trying to figure him out. I had more important things to think about.

Like, what was Elizabeth doing? Was my father still fighting to live? I hadn't drunk the potion, so I figured I would know when he finally . . . when he *died*. I'd feel it and more than likely, from what I'd gathered, I'd be summoned to the castle where I'd be stuck until I died. Which, if Elizabeth had anything to do with it, would be about ten minutes later.

"I don't understand what you're talking about," I said. "Dangerous history? Being a Darkling is like having a birth defect, I think. I'm lucky to have lasted as long as I have."

He took that in and studied me for a moment longer. "Actually, that couldn't be farther from the truth. Darklings are powerful, scary creatures if not taken care of properly." He shrugged. "Considering that they're made up of two of the scariest, most unpredictable creatures in the universe—demons and humans—this is not difficult for me to believe. It's one of the many reasons why human/demon relationships are forbidden—"

"Forbidden?" I didn't know that.

He nodded. "It's strictly forbidden. So we don't have a bunch of dangerous Darklings running amok."

I frowned. Powerful, scary creatures? "How do you know this?"

"It's my duty to know these things—to be advised about my enemies. Everything I do and learn is to keep my land safe from those who might do us harm." He took another step closer until we were almost touching. "I expected such darkness from you, Nikki. But I sense nothing but light. This is very strange, indeed. I need to consider this."

"Does that mean that you'll help me?" I asked hopefully. "You don't want Elizabeth ruling the Shadowlands right next door. She's evil."

"She is that. But she is a demon, so it's not exactly unexpected, is it?"

"My father isn't evil."

"Your father"—Rhys paused—"is still a demon and unpredictable by nature. He will do what is necessary to achieve his goals, no matter the cost."

Frustration welled inside of me. "He's dying. And you could help me save him."

If the king of the faery realm would help me out, maybe I didn't have to go back to my world just yet. I could stop Elizabeth. I could demand that she give me the antidote . . . that is, if she hadn't destroyed it already.

I didn't even want to consider that possibility.

I had to remind myself that all was not lost. Everything could still turn out okay. I felt a ray of hope shine through my fear.

"I'm not helping you," Rhys said. "Even though the Shadowlands is an important barrier for us, it is not our only option for safety and self-preservation. Faeries have nothing to do with demons . . . and *especially* not Darklings. Ever."

"But—"

He held up a hand. "Is that the real reason why you entered my forest, Nikki? To ask for my help? Or is it something else entirely? Are you using a spell to hide your darkness from me? To try to trick me, to take my land, destroy my people?" His calm façade was slipping a little and there was a glittering in his eyes that was anything but friendly. "Because I'd strongly advise against that."

Was he serious? "No, of course not. I'm just hiding here."

"A Darkling would never have to hide from anyone or anything." His eyes narrowed. "And how you were able to touch the unicorn is curious to me. Your magic must be very strong to trick a creature like that. They are repelled by anything remotely impure or . . . *demonic*."

I narrowed my eyes as well. "Maybe that should tell you something. I'm *not* one of the bad guys."

"Perhaps." His lips curled to the sides and his gaze swept slowly over me again. "You're definitely not what I expected. But it doesn't change the fact that you've still trespassed onto my land. You've touched one of my unicorns. The penalty for that is death."

I shook my head, the new swell of fear making my head ache badly. I glared at him. "Get away from me."

A trace of fear moved behind his eyes and he took a step back. I wondered for a moment if my eyes had turned demon red. "Are you going to take Darkling form to defend yourself from me?"

I frowned hard. "I . . . I don't know. Maybe I will."

He pressed his lips together, any friendliness on his handsome face only a memory now. "Whatever magical deception you've created here has also worked on me. I find that I like you, Nikki, despite what I know you are. Maybe I'll let you live if you get out of my forest in the next ten seconds and promise to never return. Do you agree?"

My headache eased slightly. If he liked me, maybe I could still convince him to help. "But, Rhys . . ."

He drew a sword out from a sheath on his back and pointed it in my direction, almost touching my throat. My eyes widened in shock. "Ten," he began. "Nine . . . eight . . ."

He wasn't kidding.

I turned and ran away from the king of the faery realm as fast as my bare feet could carry me. I cleared the last tree when I heard him get to "two" and then I didn't hear anything after that, but I kept jogging with my attention over my shoulder, waiting for a swarm of angry faeries to come flying out after me.

But there was nothing. It was a huge relief.

That guy was crazy. Territorial. And completely impossible to talk to. And he was the king? I felt sorry for the other faeries.

Out of everything he'd said, the one thing that confused me the most was the part about Darklings being fearsome creatures. For that brief moment, the cocky Rhys had looked at me with fear in his eyes.

He was afraid. Of *me*.

More like the other way around. That sword had been very sharp. As I slowed down, I thought about it. Why did everyone want to kill me all of a sudden? I stopped and put my hands over my face, suddenly overwhelmed by everything. I was trapped there. Without having a gateway to get back, there was nowhere for me to go. There was the faery realm—obviously off-limits for me now. There was the clearing—not exactly the best place to hide. And there was Castle Dread—the only part of the Shadowlands that looked like anything other than a whole lot of nothing. Far beyond were the jagged mountains that apparently bordered the rest of the Underworld, but it was so far away I'd never be able to walk there, and I was pretty certain that it wasn't somewhere I wanted to go in the first place.

I had no idea what I was going to do next. Even if I could find another gateway, what was I supposed to do? Just go back? Once I was there I had no way of finding a way to return to the Shadowlands. I knew I couldn't leave. I had to find another way.

I remembered what Elizabeth had told me earlier.

"The Underworld potion makers always create an anti-potion for everything. It's a by-product of the potion itself and a very good fail-safe—after all, one can never be too careful when it comes to magical brews."

Maybe I'd sneak back into the castle. I'd try to find the anti-potion—the antidote—to Elizabeth's poison. I'd cure my father and together we'd defeat Elizabeth.

I knew it wouldn't be that easy, but I had to try. After everything I'd learned, I couldn't simply hide.

Pushing away my fear and summoning up my remaining reserve of courage, I turned toward the castle only to find that my view was blocked.

Elizabeth's thug stood in front of me.

I stared at him, my heartbeat thudding in the backs of my eyes, in my throat, in my head.

"Princess," he said with teeth gritted together. "I never thought you'd emerge from the forest."

"I'll turn Darkling," I managed. "I can do it. You can't hurt me then."

"It will take a few moments for you to shift form." The knife turned in his grip. "I'm prepared this time."

"Did you tell Elizabeth what happened before? When I turned?"

His brow furrowed. "No."

Since Elizabeth hadn't said anything to me about it, I figured he hadn't. "Why not?"

The expression on his ugly face was grim. He was so big that he blocked out my entire view of the Shadowlands behind him with his thick body. "Do you truly think I would tell her that I allowed you to defeat me so easily? She fears you enough as it is, but if she had any idea that you'd harnessed your Darkling powers . . ." He visibly shuddered. "She would destroy me."

My entire body was tense, and I found it hard to move or breathe. "She fears me? Why does she fear me?"

"Silence." He moved the knife and I managed to stagger back a step. Instead of coming at me with it, he tucked it into a sheath at his side and pulled something else out of his pocket. A white cloth. "You have to come back to the castle with me. Your aunt wishes to speak with you."

"She wants to kill me."

"If that was the case, I would have done it already."

I looked around the empty field. Not much chance of escape that I could see. The thought made me feel ill. "What did you do to Michael?"

His lips thinned. "The Shadow is proving to be more problematic than Elizabeth ever anticipated or she would have sent him away with the other servants. He'll be taken care of in time."

He moved toward me. I stepped back and held up my hands. "Look, there has to be another way. Maybe you can help me. Aren't you sick of being told what to do? I know I was. You don't have to take orders from Elizabeth if you don't want to. That's no way to live. Maybe we can work together and figure out a way to—"

But he wasn't open to negotiations. He closed the remaining distance between us so fast I couldn't even turn around. Before I had a chance to fight back or scream, he forcibly covered my mouth with the cloth, which smelled of strange chemicals, and a few seconds later darkness claimed me.

19

I woke with a sharp sob to find my face pressed against a smooth stone floor in a cold, dark room. It took me a moment to even sit up, and when I did, I felt around, trying to establish where I was and exactly how much trouble I was in.

I was somewhere in the castle.

And I was in a whole heap of trouble.

I touched my neck. My potion bottle was missing. Where had it gone? Did it slip off my neck when Elizabeth's thug was dragging me back to the castle? Was it out in the field? Or had he taken it away from me to give to Elizabeth so she could force-feed it to me?

I was betting on the latter.

::Princess? Can you hear me?::

Michael? I drew my knees to my chest and stared blindly around at the darkness. *Where are you?*

::If you can hear me, then I must be close, but I don't know where they put us.::

I felt a sudden wave of relief at hearing from him, even if it was only telepathically. *You got away from that creep?*

::I'd hoped he'd chase me, not you. I'm sorry about that. Did he hurt you?:: He sounded upset by the idea of it.

Despite total hysteria and being scared to death, I'm still breathing. Michael, what is Elizabeth planning to do?

::I think she wants to wait for King Desmond to die and for the power to shift to you. Then she . . . then she plans to kill you. You need to get out of here. Why didn't you go through the gateway when you had the chance?::

A fist of panic clutched at my throat. *It disappeared. One moment it was there, the next it was gone.*

::Elizabeth must have discovered how to control the gateways now that the king is losing his power.::

I have to stop her, Michael. There has to be a way. I racked my brain. All of my earlier ideas seemed like huge long shots.

::You need to tell your father what she's done. About the poison. He needs to know.::

But he's so weak now. What could he do that wouldn't hurt him even more?

::He might be able to open another gateway for you. He can still help you get home.::

The room I was in was so cold I was shivering, though it wasn't just from cold—it was also from fear. I tried to calm myself down by thinking about Michael. His first thought was to protect me, to help me get home. I appreciated that so much, but I knew it was too late now. Even if I was willing to just skip back home and forget all of this, I couldn't. The moment my father died, I'd be brought back here against my will and trapped inside the castle until Elizabeth killed me to take my power. There was no turning back now.

Where are you? I thought. *I'll try to get out of here. I'll try to find you.*

There was a pause, and then, ::Princess, I have to go. I have to—::

I waited with my eyes wide as saucers for him to say something else. But there was only silence.

Michael?

There was no reply. Had Elizabeth found him?

I felt around on the cool floor until I came to a big wooden door. I got shakily to my feet, feeling for a handle, but there was none. I pushed against the door but it didn't budge. They'd locked me inside a dark room to deal with me later.

Slowly my eyes began to adjust to the lack of light until I could see. I was in a small unfurnished room. My shoes and purse were nowhere to be seen. I pushed on the door again, attempting to use my shoulder as leverage but it was impossible.

I sucked in a shaky breath and looked around. There had to be a way out of here. Michael was right. The only thing I could do now was to find my father and tell him about Elizabeth and pray that he had enough power left to stop her.

Out of the corner of my eye I saw a soft glowing light in the darkness and I looked down. It was the crystal of my bracelet, pulsing like a tiny flashlight almost out of batteries. I frowned and ran my fingers over it.

Elizabeth had told me that it was just a regular piece of jewelry. That dragons didn't exist. That would have meant it wasn't a dragon's tear as my father had originally told me.

But I figured I'd already established that Elizabeth was a big, fat liar.

What had my father said about the bracelet? That it could help focus my powers and make them more manageable?

Elizabeth had warned that using my powers would kill me, but it hadn't. And after what Rhys had told me about Darklings being dangerous and not having to hide from anyone, I had started to realize that it might have been just one more thing she'd lied to me about.

Of course she told me if I didn't drink the potion I'd die—that had been her plan. To scare me into drinking the potion.

But I hadn't drunk it.

However, when I *had* turned Darkling I'd felt out of control, as if the Darkling controlled me instead of the other way around. But that was when my emotions were all jumbled up—fear, panic, anger. I felt all of those emotions present right then, but I wondered if things would be different if I could control them. Maybe if I concentrated, focusing on the crystal in my bracelet, it would help me channel my Darkling power.

Maybe being a Darkling was like having a muscle I never knew I had. A flabby muscle that needed to be worked on before it got strong and flexible and able to help me jump over tall buildings in a single bound.

It was definitely worth a try.

Please, I prayed inwardly. *Please let this work.*

I pressed both my palms against the door. I wanted out of that room.

Elizabeth told me that dragons didn't exist and that my father was delusional.

It hurt thinking how easily I'd been sucked into believing her. I'd liked her and I'd thought she liked me. But she didn't. She had a very specific plan and I was the only person currently standing in her way.

She was going to kill me.

The anger that flared with that thought created a sudden surge of energy and I focused all of my concentration then. The teardrop crystal lit up brightly and then both of my hands began to glow with red light. I pushed against the door and heard a splintering sound before it swung wide open.

My eyes widened. I couldn't believe it had actually worked.

I pushed my fear aside and forced myself to emerge into the hallway. I didn't know the castle at all and the hallways and corridors all looked the same to me, but I had to find Michael. And, I knew I had to find my father and tell him about Elizabeth.

Elizabeth had to be stopped in any way possible. She couldn't become queen. She planned to open the Shadowlands up to her boyfriend, and together they'd let the evil that my father had spent sixteen years holding back seep into the human and faery realms.

No matter what I had to do, I wouldn't let that happen.

I pulled Michael's sweatshirt tighter around me as I

quickly moved through passages and corridors. I turned right and left and around until I was hopelessly lost and on the verge of tears again. I'd been determined when I'd left the locked room, but the feeling had faded the longer it took me to find my way. How was I supposed to stop Elizabeth if I couldn't even find my father?

Finally I stopped walking and wiped at my damp eyes, my hands coming away smeared with what remained of my carefully applied Winter Formal makeup.

"Princess," a quiet voice said.

I turned sharply to the right. From inside a darkened room Michael stared out at me. There was a look in his eyes that almost scared me more than I already was. No, scratch that. It *did* scare me more than I already was.

But seeing him also gave me a huge sense of relief. He was all right. I'd been so scared that Elizabeth had gotten to him and had hurt him—or worse—for helping me try to escape.

"Michael." I took a step toward him. "What happened? Are you okay?"

He took a step back, holding up a hand. "Please, Princess, just stay where you are."

His expression was dark and haunted and it worried me even more. "What's wrong?"

"I'm . . . I'm a Shadow."

I frowned. "I know that already. I told you I don't care." There was something different about him, but it wasn't until I looked down at his worn, gray T-shirt that I figured it out. "Where's your amulet?"

He touched his chest with a shaky hand. "Elizabeth took it away from me."

"Why?"

"To punish me." He studied the floor at his feet. "There's no worse way to punish Shadows than to take away our amulets."

A rush of concern swept over me. "But aren't you supposed to wear it at all times? I thought you needed it."

"I do." His throat moved as he swallowed, and I noticed his eyes weren't green anymore; they were gray. "But don't worry about me. There's still a chance for you to be okay. Elizabeth doesn't want to kill you if she doesn't have to. If you drink the potion, she'll let you live."

I felt a stab of anger at what my aunt had done to him. "Would you stop protecting me for one moment and think about yourself? What happens if you don't get your amulet back?"

"Please, Princess, listen to what I'm telling you. You can go back to your normal life. Go back to school and to the dance and forget all about this."

I shook my head. "I can't do that."

"You *have* to drink the potion. Forget about me. There's no other way for you to be safe."

He sounded so broken, his voice barely a rasp as he told me to forget about him. He didn't look well at all. In addition to his eyes, his skin grew pastier the longer he stood there. He looked sick and weak and tired.

"Why do you think she'd just let me go now?" I asked. "After everything that's happened?"

"Because that's what I told him," a now-familiar voice said.

I turned to my left. Elizabeth was about twenty feet down the hall and approaching slowly. Even after everything that had happened, she was smiling warmly at me.

"Nikki," she said, "I can't begin to tell you how badly I feel about all of this. I never meant to involve you. I didn't want you to be hurt."

I looked at her, wanting to run, but not able to leave Michael behind. "How can you say that to me?"

"Because it's the truth. I don't blame you. It's not your fault that you were swept up in all of this, but it was unavoidable." She fixed me with a concerned look. "I tried to make it easy for you. I wish you'd never learned the truth."

"The truth that you're murdering my father?"

Her shoulders stiffened. "You make it sound so horrible."

"How is it not horrible? How is there anything about it that *isn't* horrible? You're poisoning your own brother. How can you do that?"

She ignored my question. "How did you escape from your room? I know it was locked very well."

I used my Darkling strength and busted it open, I thought. But I didn't say it out loud.

Michael, I projected telepathically, *what's wrong with you? What has she done to you? Please tell me.*

There was no reply, even though he was standing six feet away from me.

"You didn't answer me," I said to Elizabeth, trying as hard as I could not to sound scared to death. Her casually polite demeanor was now scary rather than pleasant. "Why are you doing this?"

She spread her hands. "The time has come for a change. The Shadowlands have been a protective barrier for so long. But who's to say that it must always be that way? I'm looking for progress instead of stagnation. My father was stuck in the old ways, and Desmond is much the same. But there are new ideas. Demons have been relegated to the dark worlds for too long. We should be given the opportunity to move out to other places if we so desire."

"Is that what Kieran wants?" I asked coolly.

She gave me a small smile. "Kieran is very wise. He knows how the worlds should be. And he loves me. Together I believe we could change the universe."

"You're insane," I said.

Her eyes narrowed at me. "Actually, I've never been more sane than I am right now," she said. "My love for Kieran has shown me possibilities other than those I was raised to believe. He has opened my eyes and helped me embrace my own potential, my own power. That is what love does, Nikki. Since you're so young, I don't expect you to understand."

I thought back to my conversation with the hot-but-creepy Kieran and shuddered. "Kieran made sure to tell me that if something happened and you didn't become queen, he and I should 'get to know each other better,'" I said, making air quotes. "And I don't think he meant because he was in love with my aunt, if you know what I mean. The guy is a jerk."

Her mouth twitched a little. "I'm sure you misunderstood him."

"No, I'm thinking that *you're* the one who misunderstood him. Did it ever occur to you that he's just using you to get to the Shadowlands? So he can take control for himself?"

"Kieran loves me," she said simply. "He's absolutely perfect. And he only wants what's best for me."

"I had a date who seemed perfect this evening," I said, flashing back to what had happened with Chris and sensing a ghost of the panic I had felt well inside me again. "He attacked me in the back of a limo."

But I could tell that she didn't want to hear what I was saying. She was so far into the decisions she'd made for the sake of true love and progress that anything else was just white noise to her.

"I'm sorry you don't understand what true love is," Elizabeth said. "I hope, for your sake, that one day you'll get the chance." She stretched out her hand and I saw that my potion bottle rested on her palm. "I took this from you to ensure that you didn't break it or dispose of it somehow. I'm giving you this last opportunity to do the right thing. Drink the potion, Nikki. Your presence has caused a disturbance in my plans, and this is your last chance to make it right."

I just glared at her.

Her expression stiffened. "Dax," she called. "Come here."

The thug came around the corner. Indoors he looked even bigger than before. He glanced at Elizabeth and then came toward me.

Instinctively I moved to where Michael stood silently and reached out to him. But as our hands would have normally touched, mine slipped right through his as if he was no more than a . . . than a . . .

. . . a shadow.

20

There was no substance to Michael. Not solid—like he was just a ghost.

His expression was pained as I looked into his now-gray eyes. "I'm sorry, Princess. I didn't want you to see me like this."

"Your amulet . . ."

"It helps a Shadow maintain solid form," Elizabeth said from behind me and chills ran down my spine. "There aren't many Shadows left after all this time. It must be horrible to have to rely on an amulet to live or die. Without it, he'll simply fade away to nothing before too long."

My eyes widened as I looked at Michael. "Is that true?"

He didn't say anything, but I could tell by the look on his face that this was one thing Elizabeth wasn't lying about.

I turned to face her. My hands were in fists at my sides. "Where's his amulet?"

She sighed. "I don't do this to be cruel, Nikki. I want you to know that. But he has been given several direct orders and he's failed me every time." She glanced at Michael. "It's almost as if he believes that you care for him as more than a servant. Or else why would he continue to protect you so single-mindedly?"

"I do care for him as more than a servant," I said fiercely. "Now give him back his amulet."

Her eyebrow raised. "Oh, I see. This is your 'somebody,' is it? The boy you think wants you to forget him, and whose true feelings are unknown to you?"

"His *amulet?*" I said louder.

"I'm afraid you're not really in a position to demand anything from me." Her expression turned graver. "But I do empathize. I know what it's like to care for somebody others feel is wrong for you—Desmond never approved of my relationship with Kieran. But you know, even if all was normal again, there is no way your father would ever allow you to be with a Shadow—it's forbidden, just as demon/human romance is. As I said before, Desmond is very set in the ways of old."

She sounded oddly empathetic for a power-hungry, murderous demon.

"I appreciate the pep talk," I said dryly.

"Oh, Nikki." Her forehead furrowed deeply. "You remind me so much of myself. I know what it's like to be a woman faced with a destiny she didn't ask for, you know. You didn't ask to be half demon. What a horrible burden to put upon someone so young. The very thought that if you harness that power you risk your own death—it's tragic, really."

She still didn't know I'd turned Darkling and had lived to tell the tale. But I wasn't telling the tale to her. It was my secret.

And Michael's. And the thug Dax's. But a quick glance at Dax's ugly but worried face told me he wasn't going to be spilling the beans anytime soon.

"Nikki," she pressed. "There's no time to continue to argue this. You have to drink the potion."

Have to.

I looked at Michael then. I didn't need telepathy to know that he wanted me to run. To get away and leave him behind.

A huge roar sounded out at that moment. A cry of pain. The sound helped me pinpoint where my father's room was—behind me and down the hall. He was so close!

Elizabeth cringed. "Why won't he stop fighting and make it easier on himself?"

Despite everything, did she feel guilty about what she was doing? She was a demon, and according to the king of the faery realm, demons were all evil. Across-the-board darkness, no exception to the rule. Even Rhys had assumed I was evil, though he didn't sense it from me. I could touch a unicorn—whatever *that* meant. So maybe Rhys was wrong.

Was there a piece of Elizabeth that wasn't that bad? She was killing her brother to please her boyfriend. But there had to be something there, something that was eating away at her. Or maybe that was just wishful thinking. She had gone too far. She'd made her decisions and I'd made mine.

I knew what I had to do.

I turned and ran as fast as I could toward the room I'd heard the roar of pain come from. I could hear Dax's thundering footsteps behind me, but he was big and heavy and couldn't run as fast as I could.

At the end of the hall, I turned right onto a long corridor and it finally seemed familiar. There was only one door. It was closed but unlocked and I burst in without knocking.

The room looked the same as before and my father still lay on the bed, but now he was curled on his side, the coal-colored skin of his forehead drenched with sweat.

"Nikki—" His voice was so weak I could barely hear it.

I ran to his side. He attempted to reach out toward me with a black, taloned hand, but it dropped back down to his side. I grabbed his arm.

"Dad . . ." I began, but realized that he'd fallen unconscious again. "No, please wake up!"

Elizabeth and Dax entered the room and Michael was right behind them. I scooted around to the other side of the canopied bed.

Elizabeth's gaze tracked to her brother and then to me. "It's too late, Nikki."

My father's eyes flickered open again and he looked up at me and then over to his sister. "Elizabeth, I am near the end. I can't fight anymore."

"No, you shouldn't fight," Elizabeth said. "But Nikki hasn't drunk the potion yet. I don't know what to say to convince her that it's for the best."

His attention moved to me. "Nikki, you must drink it. When I pass, the power of the kingdom will transfer to my heir. If you don't drink the potion, that will be you. You'll be trapped here. I want you to be happy, to take care of your mother, and not to worry about any of this."

I clung tightly to his arm. Michael and I exchanged a glance and he looked desperate. Not only for his own situation but for mine.

"I've changed my mind," I said then. "I do want to be queen after all."

Elizabeth's eyebrows shot up. "What?"

"Are you sure about that?" my father asked.

I nodded. I thought about Rhys and how he was the king of the faery realm even though he was only sixteen. "I'm sure."

"But . . . what about your normal life? What about school? Why would you change your mind about something like this?"

"Because Elizabeth *can't* be queen."

"Why not?"

I glanced at her and her eyes narrowed at me, her previously pleasant expression—even during her veiled threats—disappearing.

"Because she's been poisoning you," I told him.

Elizabeth's mouth dropped open. Did she really think I wasn't going to say anything?

I kept talking. "Every time she brings you water it has poison in it. She's been trying to kill you. She wants the throne and she'll do anything to get it."

Elizabeth underestimated me if she thought the lure of going back to my regular life and forgetting all about this would be enough to deter me. How shallow did she think I was?

I didn't want this. But if she thought she could take the throne and destroy everything my father had achieved— even at the expense of giving up his happiness with my mother—then she had another thing coming to her.

In fact, I'd made this decision earlier at the dance— even before I realized what Elizabeth's nasty plan was. I just hadn't realized how strongly I felt about it. All I knew was that it felt right to me—even if it meant going against what everyone else wanted me to do.

And if the power of the kingdom shifted to me and Elizabeth tried to kill me? Then she would have one hell of a fight on her hands.

"Elizabeth," my father said, and even though his voice was weak, the name still held power. "Is this true?"

She came to his side so we looked at each other over my father's prone form. "Of course not. I don't know what has gotten into her, but your daughter is completely wrong. Why would I want to harm you? You're my brother."

"It's true," Michael said from the edge of the room. He had his arms crossed over his chest now and was visibly shivering even though the room wasn't cold. "Elizabeth has been poisoning you so she and Prince Kieran can share the power of the Shadowlands."

"You're still seeing that devious Underworld prince?" My father's eyes shifted back and forth quickly as if he was thinking very hard. "No. Elizabeth, I . . . how could I be so horribly blind?" His forehead creased and his brows drew together. "Why would you do this to me? I trusted you. Above all others in this world, I trusted you. You would watch me suffer these weeks and say nothing?"

She backed away a step. "There was no other way. I have to be queen. Why did you bring your daughter here? She's ruined everything."

My father was struggling to sit up and a flash of fear crossed Elizabeth's expression. However, despite his fierce demon exterior it was apparent that he had no strength left at all. He couldn't do anything to stop her. The poison continued to eat away at his remaining life.

She looked at me then, and her eyes turned to red. "You leave me with no other choice, Nikki. You could have made this so simple. Two sips at the most and none of this would have mattered to you. I'm not as horrible as you probably think I am. I've done what I had to do, but no more than that. I didn't want to kill you."

I willed myself to remain calm. My father was staying conscious but I could tell that it was a struggle.

"I think you've deluded yourself into thinking you're better than you really are, Elizabeth," I said.

Her eyes narrowed. "Right now you are vulnerable. If I wait until the power shifts to you, you won't be. This is my only opportunity to make things right."

"Nikki," my father said, "I can't protect you. I'm too weak."

"Then I'll have to protect *you*." My grip increased on his arm and I glared at my aunt. "Forget it. Not going to happen." I glanced at Dax, who stood expressionless by the doorway with his arms clasped behind his back. He looked like a bouncer.

I could feel Elizabeth's desperation and her growing anger like a crackling of heat along the surface of my skin. There was the briefest flash of her demon then. It scared the hell out of me. I'd almost forgotten that she also had a demon form just underneath the surface of her beautiful human exterior.

"I think I know what to do," she said after a moment and I watched her apprehensively as she reached into the pocket at the side of her skirt and pulled out Michael's amulet, holding it up by its chain. I felt the air leave my lungs in a rush.

"You do know what this is, yes?" she asked.

"Of course I do." I was literally trembling from trying to sound strong when I felt anything but.

"Your Shadow can't help you now, Nikki, but perhaps you can help him."

Michael had become so transparent that I could see through him to the wall behind. By how pale and shivery he was, I could tell he wasn't feeling very well. Being without his amulet had damaged him. It contained his life force, his ties to the world. Without it he was . . . nothing.

Elizabeth waited for me to say something but my mouth had gone so dry that I didn't think I could have formed words even if I wanted to.

So she continued, her voice tense. "Please listen to me, Nikki. I know you care about him. Drink the potion and I will give this amulet back to Michael. If you refuse, then he will continue to fade away until he has completely disappeared from our sight. Even then he'll still exist. He'll be invisible to the world around him, but in desperate, constant pain for many years until he finally dies. It is a horrible end to give somebody you obviously have feelings for. I can't imagine that you'd ever want him to suffer so greatly."

I looked down at my father then, tearing my attention away from Michael's fading form, and saw that his breathing was growing more shallow and his eyes were closed. He had slipped unconscious again. When I looked at Michael I could see the raw desperation on his face.

"Don't listen to her," he said. "Forget about me."

Forget about him. I didn't think I could. Not ever. I felt changed, and not just because I had discovered my Darkling side. It was something deep inside of me that didn't want the people I cared about to be hurt if there was anything I could do about it.

I'd tried to be strong even though I was quivering inside. I'd tried to be brave. But I didn't think I could do it anymore. A tear trickled down my left cheek, betraying the emotional breakdown I was feeling inside.

"I need a decision," Elizabeth said. "Please, Nikki. The time has come."

She thought she was giving me a choice. Let Elizabeth rule in my father's place or condemn Michael to years of torture.

But I'd already made my choice. I couldn't turn back now.

21

"Don't do it, Princess." Michael drew closer but it only helped me to see the pain he was going through. "Please . . . let me go. Your father wouldn't want you to sacrifice the kingdom for me."

"First you want me to drink it." My voice broke a little as I said it. "Now you say don't drink it. You've very indecisive, do you know that?"

"That was when I wanted you to save yourself, not me." He gave me a very weak smile. "Don't drink it. I'm not important."

I blinked back more tears. "You're important to me."

He reached out to me and our fingers passed right through each other. I felt nothing at all, not even a glimmer of energy from him. It was much worse than getting a jolt of electricity from touching his amulet by mistake. This . . . this *nothingness* was much worse.

I wondered if I could grab Elizabeth then and take the amulet away from her, but another glance at Dax showed me that he now held it. Besides, the brief glimpse of her demon earlier had proven to me that she wasn't just a pretty blonde in a long red gown. She was powerful and scary and, at the moment, *desperate* for me to do what she wanted no matter what the cost.

Elizabeth held up the little bottle to me and I took it from her without another word.

My father's eyes flickered open again and he sucked in a breath of air. "Elizabeth, you must stop what you're doing while you still have a chance. It's not right. You can't make Nikki do this if she doesn't want to."

"It *is* her choice," Elizabeth said. "I'm sorry, Desmond. I truly am. But this is the way it has to be."

Has to.

"Nikki . . . ," my father managed.

I held the cool bottle in the palm of my hand, my cheeks wet with tears. "When Michael first told me I was half demon, I didn't believe it. I thought he was crazy. I had to see it with my own eyes and when I did it nearly scared me to death. I just wanted to fit in at school. I didn't want to be a demon princess and I sure didn't want to become queen of the Shadowlands."

"I know," my father said. "That's why I had the potion made for you."

"I could see that you were a little disappointed that I took the bottle from you so quickly. That I wanted to forget."

"It's the way it must be," he said. "The choice has always been yours, not mine. Not Elizabeth's. Even now, Nikki, the choice is yours."

The magic potion had been the perfect solution to all

of my problems. But I'd had some time to think about it since he'd first given it to me. I'd thought long and hard about what my choices really were—even beyond the threat that turning Darkling would kill me. And I had already made my decision of what to do.

For better or for worse, I was still certain it was the right one.

I took the top off the bottle, tipped the vial back and drank down every last drop of the red liquid. When I was finished I looked at my aunt.

Her expression was tight and her shoulders tense. She nodded. "Very good. Everything will be fine now."

I swallowed hard. "The amulet? We made a deal."

"Of course." She held out her hand and Dax came to her side to give her the amulet. "I cannot tell you how relieved I am, Nikki."

I didn't reply. I just held out my hand and she gave me the chain with the large green stone. At the moment, the stone was as gray as it had been in the alleyway yesterday afternoon. I squeezed the chain tightly in my hand. My father's expression was grim as I let go of him and moved away from the side of the bed toward Michael.

All that was left of him was a fading shimmer. Although I could see the outline of him, his clothes had become shadowy and indistinct, and the rest of him blurred. His eyes were still intently fixed on me and filled with pain.

"You should have done it to save yourself." His voice sounded miles away and strained. "But not for me. I'm nothing."

"You're *not* nothing. When are you going to start believing that?"

Michael had almost disappeared completely. How could the amulet work if it was solid and he wasn't? I reached toward him and was surprised when I could touch his arm. It must have had to do with me holding the amulet. I could still see straight through him, but his arm felt solid and very cold.

"Hold still," I advised.

"There's no time," he said again. "Your memories—"

"Don't worry about that right now." I went up on my tiptoes and slipped the amulet over his head, letting the gray stone drop down to his chest. Keeping a tight hold on his arm, as though if I let him go he'd fade away completely, I waited. He struggled to breathe and I could still see the pain in his eyes, but as I continued to watch him I saw color return to the stone a little at a time. As it did, his form became clearer and more opaque. His eyes changed from gray to green at the same speed as the amulet regained its color. I watched his handsome features fill in, the line of his arms and chest and legs. Even the Van Halen T-shirt was back and looked faded only because it was old.

After a minute had gone by I couldn't see through him at all. He was back.

I let out a great big sigh of relief and threw my arms around him, hugging him tightly against me.

That is, until his amulet gave off its old familiar, painful jolt and I jumped backward, rubbing my chest. "Ow."

His expression was strained. "Why did you have to sacrifice everything for me, Princess? You drank the potion.
You're going to forget."

"Michael, it will be fine," Elizabeth said. "I won't punish you for betraying me. You can help me in the future."

He glared at her. "I won't help you."

Her lips thinned. "You don't have any say in the matter. You're a servant."

"I release him from his servitude," my father said.
"Michael is free to do as he pleases."

"Desmond," Elizabeth gasped. "You can't do that. He's
a Shadow."

"I'm still king here." He looked up at her and there was
no kindness in his already scary expression. "And I still
make the decisions. It is unfortunate that your . . . *Prince
Kieran* . . . isn't here to help you now. I assume he's behind
all of this?"

Her mouth tensed. "It doesn't matter. You'll be gone
soon and Michael will stay here with me. The servants will
understand what's happened and they'll do as I say."

"Where is the antidote?" my father asked, his low voice
barely audible.

"It's too late for that. There's no going back now." Elizabeth turned to me. "I need you to know something. What
I said about your Darkling side killing you if you harnessed
its power—it wasn't true."

She had to feel guilty. That's what this was, wasn't it? A
woman who had done horrible things was now trying to

justify her actions. She was trying to come clean while she still had the chance. Maybe then she could live with herself.

I wondered what she'd think if she ever found out the truth about Kieran. I mean, I didn't know the whole truth, really. The only glimpse I'd had of him was a few minutes over the gazer, but I knew he didn't love my aunt. He was using her. And she'd done horrible things to gain his supposed love.

If I didn't hate her so much for what she'd done to my father, for what she'd done to me and to Michael, then I'd feel sorry for her.

She twisted her hands together. "The facts that I did research were true, but the results I told you weren't. Darklings are very powerful creatures. They were once bred to be warriors who could easily move from the human realm to the darker worlds despite any barriers there might be. Their power is pure and vast, but they became too powerful, and that's why demon/human relationships have been forbidden ever since. That's why there have been no other Darklings until you."

Michael had come over to stand at my side during Elizabeth's speech and he looked at me with concern. He was ready for me to slip into my potion-induced amnesia at any second. What was he planning to do? Pull me along like a child to the gateway? Leave me on my front porch all confused and wondering who the cute guy was who had walked me home from the dance?

"I guess Dax didn't tell you that I already knew turning Darkling wouldn't kill me," I said.

Elizabeth frowned and turned to look at her thug before returning her attention to me. "What are you talking about?"

"I appreciate the kind-and-well-intentioned-aunt act, but you're not kind or well-intentioned." I glared at her. "You can fool yourself but you can't fool me. You're horrible. You sent Dax to kill me. You don't want to kill me here, where my father can sense it, but you're fine with killing me at home. You failed. Dax failed, because I turned Darkling and kicked his butt."

Her expression tightened. "I would have liked to have known that earlier, but it doesn't matter anymore. In a few short moments you'll be—" She tilted her head to study me. "What is happening to your eyes?"

"My eyes?" I raised a hand in front of my face and saw the red glow reflecting off it, then I looked back at her. "Nothing out of the ordinary."

She looked so confused then. "What is going on?"

"I guess you could say that I have my father's eyes." I looked down at him. He, too, looked confused, but then the realization of what I had done must have dawned on him. He squeezed my hand.

Elizabeth shook her head. "I don't understand. You drank the potion. I saw you. Your Darkling should be destroyed by now. You should be forgetting everything." She looked at her brother. "The potion. Did you give her a placebo? It wasn't a real potion at all?"

"No, it was very real," he said.

I breathed out and concentrated all of my energy on my dragon's tear bracelet. My father had given it to me to help focus and control my powers. It had worked with breaking open the door to the dark room my aunt had locked me inside and it was helping me now.

My canine teeth began to elongate and sharpen. "I told you I wasn't going to drink the potion, but I didn't tell you that I'd actually made that decision earlier. You're the one who told me to trust my heart and that's exactly what I've been doing all this time. Trusting my heart. And my heart told me to flush the potion down the toilet at my Winter Formal. I filled the vial with fruit punch and that's what I just drank. When I saw it was the exact same color I decided it was fate. I'm believing in fate a lot lately."

She held a hand up to her mouth as she watched me painlessly shift to my Darkling form, an expression of disbelief and shock turning her beautiful face ugly.

My black wings unfurled behind me and I felt my father's weak gaze on me. I looked down at him. "I thought I'd hate you when I met you. But I didn't know who you really were and what happened so long ago to make you leave us. I love you and I'd never destroy the part of me that makes me your daughter."

He smiled up at me. "You make a beautiful Darkling."

"Princess, watch out!" Michael yelled.

I looked up to see Elizabeth lunging for me, her own talons extended and aimed directly for my throat.

22

Despite her initial attempts to stay calm and collected on the surface, my aunt had now brought forth her demon form to try to rip out my throat.

She grabbed hold of me and we went flying over to the far side of the room.

Her skin was now leathery, but not black as my father's was—instead, hers was a dark red. Her ears were almost as sharp as her black, spiraling horns. She glared out at me through red slitted eyes. Her chest had sunken in and I could see her ribs, as if only a skeleton was covered by the red skin underneath her dress. Her black lips peeled back from her razor-sharp teeth and she hissed at me.

While I looked half demon and half me in Darkling form, Elizabeth was definitely fully demonic—and scary as hell.

"Shouldn't have done that." Her voice was dry and edged with violence. I tried to hold her back but I felt the edge of her talons scrape against my throat. "Should have done what I said. It didn't have to end this way."

"You're evil," I managed to say through clenched teeth.

"You're only sixteen. You don't know what evil truly is."

"You know what? I don't think I ever would have been clued in if I hadn't spoken to your boyfriend," I hissed. "He's so transparent. But even then it didn't matter. I'd already flushed the potion. Where's the antidote, Elizabeth?"

Her eyes narrowed. "You're a fighter."

"If I have to be."

I managed to grab her arms and hold her back, stumbling away from the side of the bed. She was so strong. One of her talons moved to scratch my shoulder and the pain was intense, but I forced myself to ignore it. If I let my concentration slip, the next talon would go through my jugular.

And then Michael was there, trying to drag Elizabeth off of me. "Leave Nikki alone!"

His eyes flashed as green as his amulet and I could sense he was summoning power to blast her away from me, like he'd done with Dax yesterday in the park. But before he had the chance, Elizabeth whipped her head up to glare at him and with a shove she effortlessly threw him across the room. He was up on his feet in a flash and came right back at her.

"No, Michael—be careful!"

His expression was fierce as he attempted to protect me, but he was still weak from losing form earlier. Elizabeth grabbed him by his T-shirt.

"Love hurts, doesn't it?" She threw him to the side even harder than before. He hit the wall and slid down to the floor in a heap. He wasn't moving and his eyes were closed.

"Michael!" I yelled, fear twisting inside me.

I wasn't sure if he was unconscious, or injured, or . . . dead.

Elizabeth's attention returned to me. "Your Shadow is weak, Nikki. He can't protect you anymore."

My moment of distraction had given her the chance to curl her taloned, leathery hands around my throat. Her red eyes glittered.

"Let go of her, Elizabeth," my father growled. He'd forced himself up to a sitting position in his bed. "I'm warning you . . . if you harm her, you'll be the one who dies today."

Her lip curled back from her sharp teeth. "You have no power anymore, Desmond. I can't be stopped now." She shook her head. "She won't be queen. She's not capable of it—it's impossible. She's too young. Too human."

I felt the life being squeezed out of me. She was choking me.

"Please," he said, and now his words were less fierce as his strength faded again. "Let her go. I beg you, Elizabeth. Don't hurt her."

I didn't want to die. But the air was being squeezed from my body. She was so strong. Stronger than me.

I was scared.

"Darklings don't fear anyone or anything," the king of the faery realm had told me in the forest. I'd seen the fear in his eyes.

And in the field Dax had confided that Elizabeth was

afraid of me, even before she knew I'd been able to turn Darkling.

I gasped for breath, but I tried to concentrate. I tried to look past the fury and the rage I saw in Elizabeth's red eyes. I looked past it and deep inside all I could see was fear.

I clutched at her wrists and my hands glowed red. Her brow lowered. I focused a line of energy through my hands and she jumped back from me, much like I'd jumped back from Michael's amulet.

"You're afraid of me," I gasped, holding a hand to my nearly crushed throat.

"I'm not." The look in her eyes betrayed the truth. "You're the only one standing in my way. Your father can't help you. Your Shadow can't help you. Nobody can help you now."

"You're wrong." I clenched my fists. "*I* can help me."

"Dax," Elizabeth barked. "Please restrain her."

She looked over but Dax had left the room completely. I hadn't even noticed when he ran away but I wasn't all that surprised. He'd lied to Elizabeth about my turning Darkling—or at the very least, he'd withheld information from her—and he would have expected a serious punishment after that. Obviously he didn't want to stick around to see how this all played out.

Or maybe he was just sick of being told what to do.

"Elizabeth," my father said again. "Stop this now."

Michael began to stir from the floor where he lay and started to push himself up. I was so relieved to see he wasn't seriously hurt.

Elizabeth shook her head but looked a bit more uneasy than before. "I can't." Her hands began to glow with green light. "It's time, Nikki. Time for me to be queen."

She raised her hand and launched a swirling ball of energy at me.

However, I'd just launched one at exactly the same time. Mine was bigger.

The two orbs of power, hers green and mine red, hit each other full-on, but because mine was larger it sent a shockwave to her side of the room that knocked her backward. She lost her footing and fell heavily to the floor.

I glared down at her. "You were scared of me because you knew all this time that I could do that, didn't you? That my power is greater than yours."

She lowered her head. "Please spare me."

I felt fury spiral inside of me and willed myself to calm down. Being Darkling brought with it a nearly uncontrollable need to destroy, and at the moment Elizabeth seemed like an excellent target. But I knew I had to calm myself down. Michael came to my side and touched my arm, and looking at him made the rage inside of me still a little.

"What should we do with her?" he asked.

"I have no idea."

"Elizabeth," my father said. "Come here."

She didn't stand up, but instead crawled to the side of his bed, refusing to meet his eyes. I could tell she felt defeated and she was acting like it. My hands continued to glow with power just in case she tried something funny.

"Where is the antidote?" he asked.

She gasped sharply. "Please, Desmond—"

"Elizabeth, I understand how easy it must have been for you to fall in love with Prince Kieran." He paused to breathe raggedly. "I, too, fell in love with someone who was forbidden to me. It didn't make the love any less important. Listen to me. Give me the antidote. If you do this, all will be forgiven. I will let you continue to live here in the castle with me and there will be no punishment."

I touched Michael's arm. Was he serious? After everything she'd done he was willing to forgive her?

Elizabeth's demon eyes widened. "Do you speak the truth, brother?"

"I do."

She slowly got to her feet. "I didn't know that the poison would cause you such pain. I thought it would act quicker. I'm sorry for that."

His gaze was fixed on her. "It's fine. It's over now."

She took in a shaky breath and let it out, and I watched as her demon form faded away and she became human again. It was easier to see her expression now. She was crying. She reached into her left pocket and pulled out a small clear bottle.

"Is that it?" my father asked.

She nodded.

"I'm surprised you didn't destroy it," he said. "Obviously some part of you knew what you were doing was wrong, and you wanted the chance to fix this. Please, give it to me."

She uncorked the bottle and held it to his lips. "It might be too late."

"We shall see." My father drank the antidote and closed his eyes.

I concentrated on staying in Darkling form and stood at the end of the bed, vigilant to whatever happened next. I didn't want to hope for a miracle, but that's what I was praying for anyway. Elizabeth's hands were shaking as she placed the now-empty bottle on the bedside table.

For all I knew she could have just given him a full dose of poison. If that was the case then I was afraid of what I would do to her. I wasn't ready to forgive. Not yet. Probably not ever.

It took ten full minutes before we could see any change in my father, and even then it was slow and subtle. My father's form began to change in the bed and become smaller, shifting slowly back to human. I went to his side to hold his hand, and after another five minutes he opened his eyes and looked up at me.

"I'm so proud of you, Nikki," he said.

"Are you . . ." I swallowed. "Are you going to be okay now?"

"The magic of the potion makers works very quickly," he said. "But the poison did a great deal of damage to me. It will take some time for me to fully recover. But I think I'll eventually be okay."

"I'm very glad to hear that," I said and smiled. "Because I *really* didn't want to be queen. Like, *at all*."

"I didn't think so."

My concentration had lapsed and I felt my Darkling slip away with the oh-so-pleasant sensation of a hundred Band-Aids being ripped off my brain simultaneously. I staggered, but Michael was there to catch me. I looked at him gratefully as I leaned against his solid form.

"I trusted you," my father said, and I realized he was speaking to Elizabeth. "And you betrayed me."

She didn't look at him. "I'm sorry."

"Your love for Kieran must be very great."

"I thought it was." She swallowed. "But perhaps Nikki is right. It's possible that he may have been using me."

"Do you really think so?" my father asked calmly, but the edge of sarcasm in his voice made me realize that he was anything but calm. I noticed then that despite his human appearance his eyes were red again. "Let me ask you this, Elizabeth. Our father—did you kill him as well?"

She didn't answer for a very long time. "During my first visit to the Underworld I fell in love with Kieran, even though we were very young. Our father refused to let me go back to see him again. He was a horrible, cruel man. Kieran suggested that something could be done about it. He sent me the potion."

"You mean, the *poison*," my father corrected. "Nikki, Michael, please help me get out of this bed." We supported him so he was able to swing his legs out and get to his feet. His chest was bare but he wore loose-fitting black pants.

Elizabeth shied away from him as he approached. "You said that you'd forgive me and I could continue to live here."

"I did say that. But I've been rethinking my decision. What you've done is unforgivable, Elizabeth."

Her expression grew worried. "Maybe in time—"

He held up a hand that glowed red. "You've said enough. You killed our father, you tried to kill me, and you tried to kill my daughter."

"Darklings are unpredictable," she said. "They're dangerous."

"So, apparently, are sisters."

She breathed shakily. "What will you do with me? Imprison me? Kill me?"

"I've considered those options."

Tears streamed down her cheeks. "Kieran will be very angry if anything happens to me. He will avenge me if you lock me away somewhere alone."

"Yes, well." His jaw tightened. "I wanted to spend these past years with the woman I loved instead of a solitary existence in this castle. But I would never wish the same fate on you." His eyes narrowed. "Let your prince deal with you. See if he still loves you when you offer him nothing but your constant presence."

"Desmond, please!"

"I'm banishing you to the far reaches of the Underworld. You will never return to the Shadowlands."

Her eyes widened. "No, you can't—"

"Good-bye, Elizabeth." He thrust a hand at her and a

red stream of power hit her chest before enveloping her. She screamed and in the very next instant had disappeared completely. The room crackled with power and it made the fine hair on my arms stand straight up.

I sucked in a breath. I'd never seen anything quite like that before—both the disappearance of my aunt and the rage in my father's face which quickly faded now that she was gone.

My father let out a long sigh. "I'm sorry it had to end that way." He turned to me. "And I'm sorry you had to witness that."

I hugged him then. Tightly. "Is it mean that I was hoping you weren't just going to forgive her after what she did?"

"I didn't want to lie to her, but I was desperate to get that antidote." He sighed. "I cared for my sister. She had me completely fooled. I still can't believe what she tried to do."

I glanced at Michael, who stood to the side, his eyes on the ground. My father looked at him as well.

"Thank you, Michael, for your help," my father said. "You may leave us now."

"Yes, Your Majesty."

I went to Michael's side and stopped him before he took a step. "He risked his life to help you and that's all he gets? A 'thanks for your help you can leave now'?"

My father looked confused. "I don't understand."

I felt mad, then. After the roller coaster of emotions I'd just been on, from scared to relieved to happy, now I was falling straight down the steep hill into mad. "That's the problem. You *don't* understand."

"It's fine, Princess," Michael said.

"No, it's not." I turned back to my father. "Before, you said that he was free. That he didn't have to be a servant anymore."

"I did say that." My father blinked. "And I stand by it. If you wish to leave the castle, Michael, I won't stop you."

Michael didn't say anything for a moment. "I have nowhere else to go."

"You are also welcome to stay," my father said. "I will need help to regain my strength and to summon the rest of my servants back."

He nodded. "Then I'll stay. Thank you, Your Majesty."

"But not as a servant," I said.

They both looked at me.

"He really helped us," I continued. "He protected me. If it wasn't for him, Elizabeth would be picking out her new crown right now."

"Nikki," my father began, "while I appreciate all that Michael has done, he is a Shadow. And Shadows are servants. That's just the way it is."

"Doesn't have to be."

His mouth twitched into a small grin. "Two days with knowledge of this world and she's all ready to change the politics here. But things that have existed for millennia cannot be changed in two days."

"But you'll make an exception for Michael," I persisted.

His smile faded as his expression darkened. "If I didn't know better I'd say that there was something between you.

But that would be forbidden. Humans and demons are not supposed to become romantically involved and neither are Shadows and demons."

"We're not . . . like that," I said, my face flushing.

He looked at me sternly. "That is good to hear."

Is that really true? I sent the thought to Michael. *What he said?*

::Yes. It's forbidden for Shadows and demons—or *half demons*—to be together.::

So the kiss last night?

::Forbidden. Very, very forbidden.::

Sounds like a play I had to read in English class, I thought.

::What play is that?::

Never mind.

"So you being with my mom was forbidden," I said after a moment, looking directly at my father. "But you did it anyway."

"I was young and foolish and willing to break the rules no matter the consequences." He pulled on a black robe and tied the sash at the front. "As you know, the consequences for me were very severe."

Right. He'd been summoned here against his will and never allowed to leave—then told my mother had died. That was a severe consequence. But even if they hadn't gotten involved, he still would have been summoned back here. It hadn't been a direct punishment for breaking the rules. Just a nasty coincidence.

"Do you want me to tell my mother about all of this when I go home?" I asked. "She should know the truth after so long. And maybe I could bring her here to see you."

His face went ashy. He glanced off in the direction of the framed painting of my mother. "No, Nikki. You can't tell her. She won't understand."

"I didn't understand in the beginning, but I do now."

He shook his head. "It's best she never knows the truth and continues to think I left her all those years ago. As you said, she's moved on and found happiness. I don't want to do anything to ruin that for her."

I wasn't sure those had been my exact words. In fact, I was sure they weren't. My mother *wasn't* happy. She'd searched for love for years and come up with four lousy marriages, and I was including Robert the supreme creep in that number. Maybe if she knew my father still loved her—because I knew he still did, I could see it in his eyes—that might change. "But—"

"Please, Nikki. For me. Say nothing to her about any of this."

I sighed. This wasn't the right time, I got that. Maybe someday, but not now. "Okay, if you say so."

He frowned very hard. "I will give what you said about Michael some thought. I suppose, in the meantime, I am willing to hold true to my promise to free him from his regular servant status but allow him to stay on here at the castle as a . . . a paid employee. Would that be better?"

I looked at Michael. *Is that okay with you? I mean, it's not perfect, but it's better than nothing.*

He smiled. ::It's a start.::

I approached my father. "Thank you."

"Will you visit me again?" he asked.

"On a regular basis. I'm still a Darkling, after all, and I do have these powers to deal with. These potentially dangerous and destructive powers, according to several sources. And it's not like I can just talk to anyone about them." I hesitated. "But I don't know how to find a gateway without Michael always being there."

He touched the crystal on my bracelet. "Concentrate and you'll find one. This will lead the way for you. Practice will make it easier." He placed his hand against the side of my face. "You should probably go home now or your mother will be worried."

I threw my arms around him and hugged him tightly. I'd always imagined what my father would be like—a good-for-nothing creep who'd left my mother when she was pregnant and vulnerable. But he wasn't like that at all. He was nothing I'd ever expected him to be.

He was a demon king who ruled over another dimension. Who held back the evil from the Underworld and Hell so my world would be safe from harm.

He was fairly awesome, actually.

"Please take care of yourself," I said. "Like, regular exercise, good diet. You need to live for a very long time."

He laughed. "That's right. You didn't drink the potion after all, did you? You're still my heir. If it's any consolation, demons are known to live for a very, very long time."

"Still. An apple a day can't hurt."

"I will keep that in mind." He touched my shoulder. "I'll see you again, Nikki. Soon."

I nodded and wiped away a tear. "Definitely."

23

A little while later Michael and I left the castle and headed back toward the grassy area. I saw my discarded shoes and purse and picked them up, taking a moment to put the strappy heels back on. I'd had a scratch on my shoulder from Elizabeth's talons, but it had disappeared when I'd turned back to human again. A quick inspection of my dress confirmed that, other than a small grass stain on the bottom hem, it was miraculously undamaged.

I thought I'd had trouble dealing with Elizabeth's wrath? I didn't want to have to face my mother's for ruining her Versace dress. Talk about demonic.

Michael was quiet on our way to the gateway, which was shimmering where it had been before. I wondered if he was thinking about his new status at the castle. I didn't know if it would change anything, but I hoped that my father would start treating him with a bit more respect. It was the very least that he deserved.

I couldn't believe that only a couple of days ago I'd seen him across the cafeteria watching me and had been scared by him. Then again, staring at somebody for ten minutes without saying anything *was* a bit strange. Also, following them into a park after dark wasn't the best way to make a good first impression, either. But I'd long since forgiven him for our rocky start.

"Hey, are you okay?" I asked when we reached the gateway.

He nodded, and raised his gaze to mine. His eyes were vibrant green again, even more so in the bright light of the clearing. "I'm fine. Here . . ." He peeled off his sweatshirt and draped it over my shoulders. "It's going to be cold back there. Come on."

He walked through the gateway and I followed him. There was the sudden lurch, the sensation of vertigo, and then I was back home on the dark, chilly street where my house was. I knew I'd left the dance at about eight thirty, and I figured I'd been in the Shadowlands for a few hours at least. It had to be around midnight. The same time I would have been coming home from Winter Formal if it had been just a regular night.

When we got to my house, we stopped by the maple tree and I looked at him. "Tell me what's wrong."

He shook his head. "I've been thinking about what your father said. He reminded me about the rules. All this time I've been thinking that you're the princess and I'm just a servant. I forgot about the bigger problem."

"The Shadow/demon thing?"

He wasn't looking at me. His green amulet glinted under the street lamp. "I like you, Princess. I like you so much, but there are too many problems. I don't want you to have to deal with this." His expression tensed. "Not that I'm saying you *want* to deal with this, at all. I mean, it's not like we're together, or anything." He covered his face with his hands. "I think I need to stop talking now."

I bit my bottom lip, torn between feeling confused and totally elated by his little speech. "Do you have any idea how annoying you are?"

He nodded. "I know. I'm sorry."

"If you don't stop apologizing, I think I'm going to kick your butt." I crossed my arms. "And I'm pretty sure I can do it, too."

Despite himself, he grinned at that. "I'm sure you can."

There was a pause between us before I said, "Do you know that when Chris asked me to Winter Formal, I'd never been so thrilled about anything in my life?"

He glowered. "I don't think I'm going to like this story."

"I thought that this cute guy liked me and I was so happy. He was everything I wanted. Good-looking, popular, and he seemed really nice. I felt so lucky." I breathed out and watched my breath freeze in the air. "But I knew deep down there was something missing."

"What was missing?"

I shrugged. "You were."

He shook his head. "I don't understand."

"I like you, too, Michael. A lot. Too much, probably."

He raised his dark eyebrows. "Really?"

"Really." My cheeks flushed. It wasn't every day I came right out and admitted my real feelings. But Michael seemed to be the sort of guy who needed this kind of thing spelled out for him.

"But what about what your father said? It's all true. You've never known this sort of thing because you've lived around humans all your life, but there are rules that can't be broken. Shadows and demons—"

"I know what he said. And I don't really care." I let out a long sigh. "Everybody always tells me what I have to do. Well, I've decided that from now on sometimes I'm going to listen and sometimes I won't. Now, if you don't want to see me anymore, I totally understand. When I visit my father you can just make sure you're not around. But if you want to—"

He kissed me then. I wasn't prepared and I hadn't adequately puckered but it was okay. In fact, it was fantastic. I smiled against his lips as I kissed him back and hugged him against me so I could warm up a bit. He kept his hand firmly pressed against his amulet so it wouldn't shock me.

"You're freezing," he said.

"It's December."

"You should go inside."

I nodded. "I'll see you soon. Just . . . just don't tell my father."

He smiled. "You don't think he'll figure it out?"

"What's the penalty for breaking the law?"

His smile faded. "I don't know."

"Hopefully not the same as the one for touching a

unicorn." Before he could reply to that I kissed him again. "Are all Shadows good kissers?"

"I wouldn't know." He grinned. Then he took my hand in his and kissed the back of it. "Good-bye, Princess."

"*Nikki*," I reminded him for the millionth time. "And good night, not good-bye."

"Right." He kissed me one last time, tangling his fingers into my hair to pull me closer to him. "*Good night*, not good-bye. *Nikki*."

I gave him back his sweatshirt and immediately started to shiver without its meager warmth. I watched Michael walk away, my lips tingling from our forbidden kiss. I wished he could stay here and go to school with me so I could see him every day, but I knew he couldn't stay in the human realm. He had to live in the Shadowlands and I had to live here.

And we weren't supposed to like each other in the first place. If my father found out . . . he was going to be very upset.

It would have to be our little secret.

"What are you doing lurking around out here at this hour of the night?" a very unfriendly voice snapped.

I turned to my right. Robert stood in the driveway next to his Chrysler LeBaron. His right arm looked awkward in the cast and in his left hand he held a . . . suitcase?

"Where are you going?" I asked.

"Away from you."

I felt a sudden stab of concern. "Where's my mother?"

"Inside."

"What's wrong with your eye?"

Even in the darkness I could tell that a bruise was developing around his right eye. It looked puffy and sore.

"Wouldn't you like to know," he growled. "Your mother has a mean left hook on her."

My eyes narrowed and I felt my Darkling swirl inside of me. "As mean as *your* left hook?"

He glowered at me. "Some women require discipline."

I clenched my fists. "You touch my mother again and I swear to God—"

"Don't worry. I'm out of your lives forever. And I never want to see either one of you again."

"The feeling's mutual."

He didn't say anything else. He took his suitcase, his broken arm, and his bruised eye socket, got in his car, and pulled out onto the street. I watched until the car's taillights disappeared in the distance.

Then I rushed inside, feeling frozen to the bone, but overflowing with concern and curiosity. I found my mother in the kitchen pouring herself a large glass of red wine. A quick check of the wall clock confirmed that it was half past midnight.

"Oh, hi, honey," she said before taking a big gulp of the drink. "Did you have fun at the dance?" Her gaze moved down the front of me. "Is that a grass stain on my Versace dress?"

"I just saw Robert. What's going on? Did he hit you again?"

She took a deep breath and let it out slowly. "He tried

to, but I hit him first. He's gone. He's not coming back. It's over. Four strikes for me now. I don't think I'm going to get married again."

I went to her and gave her a big hug.

"I don't know what's wrong with me." Her voice was shaky. "Why can't I find somebody who'll love me and treat me right?"

"I love you."

"Thanks." She pulled back and smiled at me. "Just the two amigos, then, huh? You and me. Like it's always been."

I had a horrible thought then. "Does this mean we're moving again?"

I hated the idea that we would have to leave and go somewhere else to start all over again. I'd lived so many different places and finally, despite my problems with Chris, I was somewhere I wanted to stay. I valued Melinda as a friend. I liked my classes. I even liked some of my teachers.

And would I be able to get to the Shadowlands from anywhere? How did that work? I didn't know and I couldn't leave until I knew for sure.

She shook her head. "I'm sick of moving around so much. Besides, you know I grew up near this area. I think I've finally found my home again. We'll stay in Erin Heights for a while, anyway. At least until you finish high school. Is that okay with you?"

I felt a surge of relief. "That's definitely okay."

"How did things work out with Chris?"

I grimaced. "Not so well. I won't be seeing him again."

"I'm sorry, honey." She stroked the hair back off my

face and tucked it behind my ear. "Maybe one day we'll both get to have our happy endings."

"I thought you said that was only in your books."

She shrugged. "Maybe I was wrong. Life is full of surprises, after all."

I wanted to tell her all about Michael. I wanted to tell her about my father so much, too, but I held my tongue. I'd respect his wishes.

For now.

Maybe someday I'd be able to share the truth with her, both about me and about him. There was a reason he had a painting of my mother on his wall—a reason he wanted to protect her from the truth about him. It was because he'd never forgotten about her. Because he still loved her. Maybe that's the reason she'd searched so hard to find love but it had never worked out. Because *my father* was the perfect man for her.

Even though he was a demon.

But then again, so was I. Half demon, anyway.

I'd always believed that demons were evil, but my father wasn't evil.

I wasn't evil.

However, there was one person who might disagree with that statement. Chris had seen me in full Darkling form. I was willing to bet that he'd stay very far away from me from this moment forward.

That was just fine with me.

But would he tell anyone what he saw? Was my secret safe? I didn't know for sure.

Everything was going to be okay, though. I could feel it. And if it wasn't, then I'd have to do something to make it okay because no one better mess with me or anyone I loved.

After all, mess with the demon and you get the horns. Cute horns. But still, *horns*.

*For Nikki Donovan, demon princess,
navigating the Underworld is a piece of cake—
it's navigating the hallways of her high school
that's hellish.*

Don't miss the second installment
in the wickedly fun Demon Princess series

COMING
SPRING
2010

Demon Princess

REIGN CHECK

Turn the page for a sneak peek!
I dare you . . .

1

Act normal, I told myself as I pushed through the front doors of Erin Heights High School. *Everything's going to be just fine.*

That thought lasted exactly thirty seconds. Then I saw Melinda, my best friend, waiting for me by our lockers. The look on her face immediately made me nervous. She looked way too excited about something.

It was eight thirty on a Monday morning and freezing cold outside. The roads were sheets of ice that only looked like roads. Everything else was blanketed in thick snow. Christmas vacation was still a whole week away. Obviously, in my opinion, there was nothing to get all that excited about.

It was probably nothing. But I couldn't help being on edge. After all, I now had a secret that nobody, including Melinda, could find out.

A week ago, I was a normal, boring teenager.

Then I met my father for the first time and found out he was a demon. And not just any demon: he was also the king of another dimension called the Shadowlands.

Which made me a princess—a *demon* princess.

So very *not* normal.

That was the secret I now had to keep from everybody.

After all, I didn't live in the Shadowlands; I lived here, in the real world. With homework, crabby teachers, and a curfew.

Not that anyone would believe me if I actually told them the truth. It sounded all kinds of crazy, didn't it?

I approached Melinda warily. I hadn't spoken to her since Saturday morning—during a quick ten-minute phone call in which I pretended I was sick to get out of going to the mall with her. I'd been recovering from my near-death experience in the Shadowlands, when my demonic aunt Elizabeth had tried unsuccessfully to kill me and my father so she could take over the throne. The fact that I wasn't up for a few hours of shopping the next day didn't make me a bad friend—just one who needed to sleep in as long as possible.

This morning the blonde, model-pretty Melinda looked as perfect as she always did. She was the queen of the "Royal Party," which is what some of the most popular kids at Erin Heights were called.

"Nikki!" Melinda greeted me enthusiastically.

"Hey, what's going on? You look like you're ready to explode."

"There's a new guy starting today in our grade," she said. "Wait till you see him. He's *gorgeous*."

"New guy?" I repeated. "That's why you look like you just won the lottery? There's a new student. Big deal."

She had a serious perma-grin thing going on. "I think I'm in love."

I relaxed a bit. Happily, this seemed to be an issue that had nothing to do with me. I could definitely deal with any new student Melinda thought was hot.

Not a problem.

I shifted my heavy backpack to my other shoulder. "I thought you only liked older guys."

She shrugged. "I'm making an exception to my over-sixteen rule. Rumor has it he's a foreign exchange student, but he doesn't have an accent."

"You've talked to him?"

"Not yet. But Larissa bumped into him and he said 'Excuse me' and asked for directions to the principal's office. She's so lucky."

I tried to refrain from rolling my eyes. Larissa and I didn't get along that well. "That's definitely one of the words I'd use to describe her."

Melinda worked on the combination to her locker and swung it open.

"Nice crown." I nodded at the top shelf inside.

"Thanks. I want to keep it close. It makes me happy." She ran her fingers over the shiny silver plastic headpiece tipped with snowflakes. She'd been crowned Winter Queen last Friday night at the school's formal dance. "I'm still dying to know how everything went with you and Chris, you know. You guys left so early and I haven't seen you since."

With that, she gave me a huge grin, as if she thought Chris Sanders and I were soulmates and she was taking the credit for setting us up in the first place. Which, admittedly, she kind of did.

"There's really not much to say," I began, trying to think of a way to change the subject as quickly as possible.

Melinda looked over my shoulder. "Oh, here he comes now. Hey, Chris!"

I froze and slowly turned around.

Chris Sanders stopped walking, right in the middle of the hallway, and his eyes widened a little when he saw me. He was just as good looking now as the first time I'd seen him when my mom and I moved here two months ago—all tall, broad-shouldered, and blue-eyed. I'd developed an immediate crush on him. I had been so thrilled when he'd asked me to Winter Formal, you have no idea.

Funny how things changed.

"H-hey, uh, Melinda." Chris stuttered the greeting in an awkward manner that majorly conflicted with his usual confidence. "And . . . Nikki . . . um, good to see you."

I pasted a frozen smile on my face. "Yeah . . . you too."

Melinda looked at us each in turn, confused.

Then again, she didn't know what happened between Chris and me when we left the dance early. My perfect crush had too much to drink, he'd cornered me in the back of an empty limousine, and tried to . . . well, let's just say he tried to do something I didn't want to do.

When I got mad or scared or stressed out, I unconsciously tapped into my demon side. We're talking black leathery wings, horns, talons, extra strength, the works. A teenaged she-demon who could kick butt.

I'd . . . sort of kicked Chris's butt.

Well, he totally deserved it.

Unfortunately, he now knew my secret. I was really, really hoping that he'd convinced himself he'd imagined it all. I mean, he *was* pretty drunk.

"You're coming to my Christmas party on Saturday night, right?" Melinda asked after a long, uncomfortable moment of silence passed among us in the busy hallway.

Chris nodded stiffly. "Wouldn't miss it."

"You have to choose a Secret Santa name for the gift exchange. So do you, Nikki."

The frozen smile on my face was starting to cramp. "Sounds like fun."

"Yeah," Chris agreed halfheartedly. For a moment I thought he was going to leave without another word, but instead he looked directly at me. "Nikki, I . . . I want to talk to you."

"Now?" I squeaked.

I really hated it when I squeaked.

"No, but soon. Really soon. It's important." He nodded firmly, his jaw tense, and then he walked away.

He wanted to talk to me. About what?

Like I had to ask.

I could deal with him. *Sure*. I'd just convince him that he'd seen things. Spiral-horned, black-winged, red-eyed things that threw balls of energy in self-defense. While wearing a fancy dress and high heels.

Sure. No problem.

Melinda looked perplexed by this exchange. She glanced at me. "He's acting strange. What was that all about?"

"I have no idea," I lied.

"Aren't you two together anymore?"

"*Anymore*? Were we together in the first place?"

"You went to the dance together."

"So?" I tried to look innocent. It was difficult. "Does that mean I have to marry him or something?"

She finally smiled again. "Yeah, you have to marry him. Didn't you know that? Going to Winter Formal means you're automatically engaged."

I couldn't help but snort a little at that. "Then we're in serious trouble."

She sighed. "It's too bad. I thought you and Chris would be perfect together. Are you interested in somebody else?"

I looked at her cautiously. "Why? Are you going to play Cupid again?"

"Depends on who you pick."

"Nobody comes to mind."

Yet another secret I couldn't share with Melinda—or anyone else—was that I did have a boyfriend.

Michael didn't go to school here. He also wasn't exactly what you'd call a normal boyfriend. In fact, he was about as non-normal as you could get. He wasn't a human. Or a demon. He was a "Shadow" and he lived in my father's castle. Shadows were enslaved to demons and had been practically forever. It was ridiculous and outdated. From what I'd seen, the Shadowlands were seriously like something out of Medieval Times dinner theater. Only no jousting. Or turkey drumsticks.

Demons and Shadows were forbidden to be together as anything other than master and servant. *Also* ridiculous.

And get this: my father had assigned Michael to be *my* personal servant. But I didn't think of him that way at all. Plus, since Michael put his life on the line to help defeat my aunt late last Friday night, I'd made my father promise Michael wouldn't have to be a servant anymore. That was the last time I'd seen either of them.

It was all complicated enough to give me a big fat headache when I thought about it for too long. I rubbed my temples and finally opened my locker so I could unload my backpack and grab my books for the first class of the day—

biology. I had it on fairly good authority that today was dissect-a-frog day. I was looking forward to that disgusting prospect only a little more than my now-inevitable conversation with Chris.

"So your party's definitely on, huh?" I asked, trying to concentrate on something else.

Melinda nodded as she stuck her head back into her locker. "Saturday night starting at eight. Everyone's coming. Wear something Christmassy."

"Red and green color scheme. Got it."

"Chris is coming. Is that going to be a problem?"

"A problem? No, of course not."

Sure it was.

I was finding it difficult not to obsess about Chris. He was going to be a big problem. Would he tell anyone what he'd seen? And if so, what would happen then? Would I be able to deal with it?

Yes, of course I would. I'd battled my evil aunt who wanted to kill me. I could deal with Chris knowing my secret.

Still, my head began to throb.

I knew I had to keep on top of my emotions. Since I was a Darkling—half human, half demon—all this power built up inside of me since I turned sixteen, just waiting for a chance to burst free. And when your inner demon wants to burst free, it's not a pretty sight. Trust me on that.

I looked at the little mirror on my locker door and gasped. My eyes had turned red—full red with black slits for pupils, like a cat's eye. And they were glowing.

No. Not here.

I couldn't change into my Darkling form right here in the middle of the school hallway. I suddenly pictured screaming, panicked students running in every direction trying to escape from me. Yelling and pointing at the monster with the big leather wings wearing jeans and a hot pink V-neck sweater.

Relax, I told myself. *Everything's okay.*

"Can you come over earlier on Saturday and help me set things up?" Melinda's voice echoed inside her locker.

"Yeah . . . sure. No problem." I squeezed my eyes shut and attempted to breathe normally. I tried to think happy thoughts.

I thought about Michael.

Dark hair, green eyes, a rare smile.

Michael's lips. Michael *kissing me*.

Okay, I started to feel calmer. Happier.

I opened my eyes and looked in the mirror again, relieved to see they had returned to their usual hazel color. I pulled my long blonde hair back and tucked it behind my ears. A little lip gloss quickly applied from the zippered pocket of my backpack, and I was all ready to go to my first class.

I could do this. Everything was fine.

I repeated it over and over in my head.

Everything is going to be fine. Chris is my only problem this week, and I can totally deal with him.

"I guess I'll see you at lunch," I said.

"Oh my God." Melinda grabbed my arm. "Nikki, there he is."

"There who is?"

"The exchange student guy." She bit her bottom lip, her attention focused behind me. "So hot. I could die."

I turned to look and my mouth dropped open.

Melinda was right—the new guy *was* really good looking.

He was tall and cute with short chestnut brown hair. He had dark brown eyes. I wasn't close enough to see the color at the moment, but I knew they were dark brown.

How did I know? Because I'd already met the new student everyone was excited about.

His name was Rhys. He was sixteen years old. But like me, he wasn't all that normal, either.

Believe it or not, he was the king of the faery realm. The forest that bordered the Shadowlands led directly into his kingdom.

And he knew I was a demon princess.

Had I thought Chris was my only problem at the moment? Um . . . wrong. So very wrong.

The last time I'd seen Rhys, only a couple of days ago, he'd mentioned a fascination with visiting the human world someday. He'd never been here before. He brought it up during the same conversation when he'd threatened to kill me with a very sharp sword.

Out of the corner of my eye I could see Melinda's smile fade. "That's weird. Do you already know him, Nikki?"

"I . . . uh . . ." I clamped my mouth shut before I said anything that might get me into more trouble than I was already in.

Despite his death threat the last time we'd been face-to-face, the sixteen-year-old faery king was currently waving at me.

"Weird" didn't even begin to cover it.